LEABHARLANNA CHONTAE FHINE GALL
FINGAL COUNTY LIBRARIES

Items should be returned on or before the last date shown below. Items may be renewed by personal application, writing, telephone or by accessing the online Catalogue Service on Fingal Libraries' website. To renew give date due, borrower ticket number and PIN number if using online catalogue. Fines are charged on overdue items and will include postage incurred in recovery. Damage to, or loss of items will be charged to the borrower

Date Due	Date Due	Date Due
15, APR 10		
13/3/14		
2/4/14		

D0995783

Ré Ó Laighléis is a writer of adult and teenage fiction in both English and Irish. His novels and short stories have been widely translated into various languages and he has been the recipient of many literary awards, including Bisto Book of the Year awards, Oireachtas awards, the North American NAMLLA Award and a European White Ravens Award. In 1998, he was presented with the 'An Peann faoi Bhláth' award by the President of Ireland, Mary McAleese, in recognition of his contribution to Irish literature. He is a former Writer-in-Residence at the National University of Ireland, Galway (2001) and held the same post with Mayo County Council in 1999.

A Dubliner by birth, he was reared in Sallynoggin and since leaving teaching in Galway in 1992 has lived in the Burren, Co. Clare.

HOOKED

Ré Ó Laighléis

MÓINÍN

First published in 1999 by MÓINÍN
Loch Reasca, Ballyvaughan, Co. Clare, Ireland
E-mail: moinin@eircom.net
www.moinin.ie

This edition 2007

A copy of this work is available in the National Library of Ireland
and in the libraries of Trinity College, Dublin, and the
constituent colleges of the National University of Ireland.

A CIP catalogue record for this book is available from the British Library.

ISBN 978-0-9554079-3-2

Set in Palatino 10.5/13pt

This book is a work of fiction. Names, characters, places
and incidents are products of the author's imagination
and any resemblance to real persons, living or dead,
is purely coincidental.

Cover design by Raydesign

Edited and typeset by Carole Devaney

Printed and bound in Ireland by Clódóirí Lurgan, Indreabhán, Co. na Gaillimhe

By the same author

Battle for the Burren (MÓINÍN, 2007)

The Great Book of the Shapers: A right kick up in the Arts
(MÓINÍN, 2006)

Ecstasy and other stories (MÓINÍN, 2005)

Heart of Burren Stone (MÓINÍN, 2002)

Shooting from the Lip (compiled and edited)
(Mayo County Council, 2001)

Hooked (MÓINÍN, 1999)

Terror on the Burren (MÓINÍN, 1998)

An Nollaig sa Naigín (MÓINÍN, 2006)

Sceoin sa Bhoireann (MÓINÍN, 2005)

Gafa (MÓINÍN, 2004)

Goimh agus scéalta eile (MÓINÍN, 2004)

Bolgchaint agus scéalta eile (MÓINÍN, 2004)

Chagrin (Cló Mhaigh Eo, 1999)

Punk agus scéalta eile (Cló Mhaigh Eo, 1998)

Ecstasy agus scéalta eile (Cló Mhaigh Eo, 1998)

An Taistealaí (Cló Mhaigh Eo, 1998)

Stríocaí ar Thóin Séabra (Coiscéim, 1998)

Cluain Soineantachta (Comhar, 1997)

Aistear Intinne (Coiscéim, 1996)

Ciorcal Meiteamorfach (CIC, 1991)

Punk agus sgeulachdan eile (Trans.) (Leabhraichean Beaga, 2006)

Ecstasy agus sgeulachdan eile (Trans.) (CLÀR, 2004)

Ecstasy e altri racconti (Trans.) (MONDADORI, 1998)

To parents

Sandra's eyes widen when she sees the array of implements stashed under Alan's bed. An old sock, she thinks, when first she pulls the bundle out. Not, indeed, that that would be much of a surprise to her. God knows, if she had the proverbial penny for every time she has pulled a dirty sock of his from under the bed over the years, she could afford to employ someone to do the cleaning for her. But, somehow, today's find is not quite the same. As she opens the cloth she mistakenly thought to be a sock, she isn't quite sure just what it is she has stumbled on. A piece of old rubber tubing, it would seem, rusty brown in colour and full of little cracks when she stretches it a little. She is bemused, totally unaware of what use it might have.

What in the name of God could it be for, anyway? And this white powder in the clear plastic bag – what's that all about? Most curious of all, perhaps, is that even the little silver spoon and the strips of meticulously folded tinsel paper don't seem to clue her to what is going on.

But then, the little chamois purse. That's when something finally registers with her: a small grey plastic syringe inside, with '2.5 ml' stamped in black on it. That rocks her back a bit all right, and even worse now is that, beside the syringe, she sees a little paper-backed plastic sachet, the seal of which is broken. A needle! Filled with fear and doubt now, she raises it to eye-level and turns it towards the window to catch the daylight. The length. The sharpness. The thought of its pointed top piercing skin and flesh sends a shudder through her. She holds the garish orange-moulded base between her forefinger and thumb, and eases the transparent plastic sheath from the needle. Naive and all though she may be, she is in no doubt now as to what it is that she has found.

Her heart jumps when she hears the opening of the halldoor below. Frantically, she shuffles the various bits and bobs back in under the bed, stands and busily takes on the appearance of one who is doing something – anything – other than that which she has been doing.

"Hi, Mam," she hears from below.

Good God Almighty, it's Alan. What's he doing home from school so early? She looks over at the clock on the bedside locker: 15.27. Something must have happened at school.

"Hello, Alan. I'm up here," she says, as she rushes out of his room and makes for the landing. Her announcement is a mixture of nervousness and guilt. "You're home early, love."

"Yeah. Froggy wasn't in today, so we had the last session free." As he speaks, he moves back out from the sitting-room and comes to the bottom of the stairs. Sandra at the top and he below. They look at each other and, immediately, Alan can see an uneasiness in his mother's eyes.

"Mr. O'Reagan, Alan. I told you before. It's just plain bad manners to call him Froggy."

"Aw, Ma, give's a break, will ya! I mean, what do you expect me to call him? After all, he is the French teacher."

"Well, how about Mr. O'Reagan, just like I said? Think of it: how would you like it if the students in your Dad's school decided to call him Hitler, just because he happens to be a German teacher?"

"Huh! I wouldn't give a hang. Sure, we call our guy Kraut and it just rolls off him. No sweat."

Alan's flippant style of talk bothers Sandra. They have

grown apart in recent times, due mainly to Alan having flunked out in all his subjects the previous year. He's repeating his final year now but, as far as Sandra can make out, it's simply more of the same. Mind you, her mindset isn't any the better for having just found that cache of stuff under his bed. She looks down at him, staring now, trying to discern something in his face that she may not have noticed up to now. Even this disregard for the teachers – Kraut and Froggy, and God only knows what else he may call some of the others – is evidence enough that there is little improvement in his attitude. In fact, if anything, he has got worse. And now, if the findings of this afternoon are anything to go by, it seems that there's even worse again to contend with.

"I'll be back later," says Alan, as he turns towards the front door.

"But what about your dinner, Alan? It's in the –"

"I'll have it later. I'll eat with Dad when he gets home," and before Sandra can protest any further, the door slams shut and he is gone. She stands statue-like in the middle of the landing, her eyes fixed firmly on the spot where Alan had been standing. She feels forlorn, inert, sensing that, if it were possible at all, she would like to be outside herself – outside her mind. That way she would not have to face the truth of what her fear is throwing up at her. And now she cries …

* * *

There is an uneasy silence at the dinner table. Dad is absorbed in the 'Irish Independent'. Even as he works the pasta with the fork, he doesn't shift his gaze from what he's reading. Naomi is seated beside him, eating and watching

'Home and Away' at the same time. And Alan, as though his life depends on successfully surpassing some eating record or other, is golloping back his food as if there is no tomorrow. And then there's Sandra, silent surveyor of this world of no communication. She is heavy-hearted, a prisoner of her own mind since earlier in the afternoon when she found much more than dirty socks under her son's bed.

"So, how were things in school today, Alan?"

"Shh!" interrupts Naomi, "I'm trying to hear this."

Brendan looks sharply at his daughter. If it weren't for the fact that she is almost thirteen, and a girl, of course, he wouldn't think twice about giving her a bloody good wallop. So, the dirty look will have to do for now.

"Don't shh me, you little Missy you, not if you know what's good for you. Do you expect me to ask your permission to speak in my own house or what?" Naomi stares back at him a second, then looks away again.

"Now, turn off that bloody box and, next time you want to watch something, you might think of showing a little manners first."

"But, Dad –"

"Off, I said, and that's that. I don't want to hear another word about it, right." And this time there is no resistance.

The telly off, Naomi sits back at the table with a face on her that's as long as a week. About as much of 'Home and Away' that she's going to see now is whatever is imprinted on her memory. The other three are quiet again too. The only thing the members of this family seem to have in common is the tension that pervades the room. Then Brendan breaks the silence once again.

"Now, Alan, how were things in school today?"

"Okay."

"Okay! What do you mean okay? That doesn't tell me

anything. What the hell is at you lately that you can't give a decent answer to anything? For Christ's sake, you'd think at seventeen years of age that you'd be able to answer a simple question," barks Brendan, and he reddens in the face. He obviously hasn't shaken off the effects of his little tiff with Naomi.

But Alan is sharp enough. He knows better than to draw his old man's temper on him.

"Sorry, Dad. A normal enough day, except that Fro ..." and suddenly he stops and looks at Sandra. "Except that Mr. O'Reagan wasn't in."

"Mr. O'Reagan. O'Reagan," Brendan muses. "That's the Maths teacher, is it?"

"No, Dad, French. Kennedy is Maths, O'Reagan is French."

"Oh, yes, yes, I remember him all right. A short stump of a guy. Yeah, I remember him gabbing on ad infinitum at some of the union meetings. Gab-gab-gab." Then he pauses. "He's the bloke they call Froggy, isn't he?"

And, with that, Alan bursts out laughing, spraying the table with the mouthful of tea he has just taken.

"Brendan!" says Sandra angrily, disappointed that his flippancy in the matter should so undermine the stance she had taken against Alan earlier in the afternoon. Alan is in kinks of laughter by now, adding to Sandra's anger and frustration. She is incensed at this naked disregard for a matter which she deems worthy of respect.

"You," she bellows at her son, "those dishes are to be cleaned before you go anywhere tonight, me boyo."

"Ah, Mam, come on."

"Clean them," she orders, no sign of softness in her voice and every bit as determined as was her husband when he had checked Naomi.

"Do what your mother tells you, Alan," says Brendan, "and, while you're at it, you can get me the telephone directory in the hallway."

Alan looks quite harshly at Brendan for a second or two, half thinking of challenging his authority. He knows that he could destroy his father if he were to reveal what he knows about him. Brendan knows that too. Still, thinks Alan, now is not the time. All things in their own good time. A silent curse will suffice on this occasion to dispel the frustration he feels at being ordered about like this by Brendan. He pushes his chair back from the table, ensuring that the wooden legs screech hard against the floorboards, then quickly makes for the kitchen.

2

There is a space between Sandra and Brendan as they lie in bed that night. It's fairly late. The clearness of the sky allows the moonlight to creep through the opening in the curtains. Sandra is quietly seething that her husband has let her down so badly earlier in the evening. But she is dealing with her disappointment in the usual fashion: silence. Just like the silence that prevailed at the dinner table. And like the silence she has kept about the gear she found under Alan's bed. She feels so alone, her back turned to her husband and her eyes focused sharply at some point on the cold white wall. Her mind is tortured by the memory of what she has come upon in Alan's room. It would be so much better for her – for everyone, perhaps – if she could just simply vent the anger that she feels towards Brendan and have that much out of the way, at least. Then, maybe, they could get around to discussing Alan.

Sandra turns now and nestles in snugly behind her husband. Somehow, it seems that it is always she who takes the first step to dissolve the tension. That in itself is no harm, maybe – submission isn't exactly Brendan's strong point and at least she has the sense to realise that someone must ultimately do what's practical. Brendan seems to be in a half sleep.

"Brendan," she whispers.

"Mmm," he says, half turning towards her, but then completely turning away from her again.

"Brendan, I'm worried."

"Mmm."

"I'm worried about Alan and what he might be up to."

"Mmm, good," says Brendan, making it glaringly obvious to Sandra that not a single word of what she is saying is registering with him.

"Brendan." This time she shakes his shoulder a little. He turns abruptly now and half raises himself off the mattress.

"For the love and honour of God, Sandra, what are you at? Can't we talk about this in the morning, whatever the hell it is?" And then he turns away again and pulls more than his fair share of the quilt in around his shoulders. She is taken aback a little by his abruptness. Quiet now. She knows better than to persist too long when he is like this, but she also realises that the matter will not simply go away, that it will have to be tackled sooner or later. Better sooner, she thinks to herself. Maybe in the morning, but then, knowing Brendan as she does, maybe not. She'll give it one more go. She's just about to place her hand on Brendan's shoulder again when she hears the front door opening. Brendan, despite the half sleep, hears it too. Suddenly, he bolts upright in the bed.

"What's that?" he asks, turning towards Sandra. He is fully alert now.

"Alan, I suppose."

"Alan!" he says, then turns towards the clock on the bedside locker. A second or two for his eyes to focus on the red neon numbers, then he looks back towards Sandra.

"Christ tonight, sure it's ten past one! Where the hell has he been until this hour of the morning?" And with that, he's up and out of the bed.

There's a right rumpus in the bedroom now as Brendan flusters about in the semi-darkness, feeling for his slippers with his feet, locates his dressing gown on the back of the door and, at the same time, switches on the light and heads out of the room. Sandra's up now too and has got to the door, but she decides it's best not to follow Brendan out onto the landing. She backs away a little and looks out through the slit between the door and the jamb. Outside, the shaft of light escaping from the bedroom makes the shadows of Brendan and his son dance threateningly on the walls.

"Where the hell were you 'til this hour?" Brendan's tone is gruff. As he asks the question, he moves across Sandra's line of vision so that all she can see is his back. She shifts a little and then so too does Brendan, and now she has a full view of Alan.

"Are you aware that it's past one o'clock in the morning, me bucko?"

Alan diverts his gaze towards the floor and doesn't answer Brendan.

"Well, I asked you a question. Where were you?"

"Out."

"Out!" Brendan's impatience is growing to anger. "Don't get smart with me, sonny, do you hear? Do you think I don't fecking-well know you were out? Do you? Now, where the bloody hell were you?"

Sandra has come closer to the slit in the door and, despite the shadowy light of the landing area, can see that Alan is nervous.

"Where, I asked you?"

"In a friend's house."

No sooner has Alan answered than he thinks that that is even less likely to satisfy his father. In fact, if anything, Brendan will more than likely misconstrue the answer and perceive it to be abrupt and brazen.

"In Cillian Reynolds' place," Alan quickly adds, preventing his father from badgering him with yet another question.

"Hmm," says Brendan, drawing a little closer to his son. "Cillian Reynolds," he says pensively.

"Yeah." There is a discernible nervousness about Alan as he utters that single word.

Brendan looks sternly at him, taking full stock of the young man's demeanour. Sandra can feel the tension mounting in her chest.

"Were you drinking?" asks Brendan.

Sandra's heart skips a beat. And, if she only knew the half of it, she would realise that so too does Alan's. Brendan is even closer to his son now, trying discreetly to get a whiff of his breath.

"Drinking?" Alan says this almost as though the question is a cause of relief to him.

"Yes, Alan, you heard me: drinking." But, by now, Brendan has already got sufficiently near to him to realise that there isn't the slightest smell of drink from his son.

Sandra's heart is racing, thumping.

"No, Dad, no I wasn't," and immediately he again looks down. He is so shrewd when it comes to handling Brendan. He knows that the sound of 'Dad' is music to his old man's ears and that, if he says it with apparent regard for him, Brendan will swallow it hook, line and sinker. And, true to form, that's exactly what happens. Brendan backs away now, seemingly happy in the knowledge that there hasn't been any drinking going on. Indeed, now that he thinks of it, if all there is to it is that Alan's a little late getting home, well, that's hardly the end of the world. Alan can see the belligerence fade from his father's face.

"Come on then, son, away to bed in the name of God. Haven't you school tomorrow, no less than the rest of us, God help us," he says, ruffling Alan's hair as he speaks, then ushering him towards his bedroom door.

Seeing this, Sandra scurries back to bed and snuggles under the quilt again, turning in to face the wall so as to give the impression that she has been lying there all the while. Her husband hangs his dressing gown on the back of the door. Then comes the dragging of his feet across the floor, the raising and lowering of the quilt and the resumption of the inevitable silence.

"Everything okay?" Sandra ventures after a while.

"Fine, fine. He was over in Cillian Reynolds' place, it seems. Listening to music all night, I suppose. Sure, you know yourself how it is with teenagers nowadays."

And then the silence again. Sandra is still worried sick by what she has come to know about her son.

No communication. No real willingness to listen on Brendan's part. Her sense of loneliness is mounting. Then, unexpectedly, Brendan decides to strike up a conversation.

"Haven't teenagers a great old time when you think of it all the same? No real responsibility as such."

But, despite her loneliness, despite the need for real sharing with her husband, Sandra doesn't answer. Her mind is far more engaged with things other than simple teenage frolics. She is engrossed in thought when Brendan starts up again. Who would credit that this could possibly be the same man from whom she couldn't get a word earlier on? To think that the very best that he could muster when she had tried to converse with him had been that irksome 'mmm' of his.

"Cillian," he muses out loud, "which of his buddies is he? Is that the tall, fair-haired young lad?"

"Yes, that's him. He's a nice lad, as far as I can tell," volunteers Sandra, responding somewhat more positively, now that she sees Brendan's effort is being sustained. "Still and all though, Brendan, it's way too late for him to be out during the school term. After all, he's only seventeen, you know."

"Ah, there's no harm in it once in a while. It's not as if he's off binging or whoring around the city centre. Bejaysus, I'm telling you, he could be doing a hell of a lot worse than sitting around listening to music. We should thank our lucky stars that that's all it is."

"Mmm," says Sandra, unable to control the intended sarcasm. And once again she feels the secrecy of what she knows creep across her mind.

"So, that Cillian – which Reynolds is he? The professor's son or the pharmacist's?"

Sandra is annoyed that the possibility of conversation seems to have so quickly reduced itself to this.

"For God's sake, don't you know right well that Professor Reynolds is a confirmed bachelor. He'd no more look at a woman than the man in the moon."

Brendan sniggers at the thought that Sandra seems to think that bachelorhood and disinterest in women go hand in hand.

"A son of the pharmacist, then. Sure, he's probably a grand lad so."

"Yeah," says Sandra, "son of the pharmacist," and her eyes widen at the thought of what all of that might mean.

3

Monday. The days are flying by and, already, the kids are on mid-term break. Even the biggest kid of all – Brendan – gets the benefit of a mid-term break. He's loafing about in the sitting-room, reading the morning 'Indo' one minute and then the 'Tribune' of the day before. He has already announced his intention of getting out of Dublin and heading down to the Midlands later in the afternoon. He'll visit his brother, John, for two or three days. A few rounds of golf, a bit of snooker, maybe, and, of course, the obligatory few pints before coming back home again.

In recent times, Sandra has found his interest in visiting John any time he gets a few days off somewhat surprising. Other than that, there's never any mention of his brother from one end of the year to the next. Not, indeed, that that bothers Sandra: she can't abide the man and is only happy that Brendan visits him rather than it being the other way round. Strange, though, she often thinks, this relatively newfound interest in visiting him.

Naomi and Alan are away off out since earlier in the morning and Sandra is busying herself about the house.

"This is the life, I'm telling you," says Brendan. He says it loudly enough that Sandra will realise that he is saying something, even if she cannot quite make out exactly what it is.

"What did you say, Brendan?"

She is upstairs – in Alan's room, as it happens. She has already cleaned Naomi's bedroom and has just now finished her own.

"This is the life, I said – free. A few days rest and freedom to do what you want, when you want, and not have to contend with those little feckers in school."

Rest and freedom. Not exactly the most prevalent elements in Sandra's life, most especially in these last few weeks. Except, of course, for some relief she has felt this past week or so. It was bad enough her finding that stuff in Alan's room some five weeks ago, but it seemed that her whole world was about to fall apart when Brendan showed so little interest in listening to her. Any time she tried to broach the subject with him, he inevitably had this or that to do and they were always things that he would 'have to see to urgently'. If not schoolwork, then it was a sports programme on TV and, if not that, the ever-present 'Independent'. Of course, her predicament was compounded by the fact that she herself was not fully au fait with what it was that she had seen. All of which was bad enough, but if, on top of that, she had had the slightest inkling of Brendan's deception, things would have seemed so much worse again.

But this past week or more has seen her overcome her state of mental flux. She is at ease about Brendan going off to spend the few days with his brother. This would not have been the case, however, if she hadn't had the time to tease the whole Alan affair out in her mind. She had made a point of checking beneath the bed on a daily basis, on some days even twice or three times. But there had been nothing there since that first day. Reflection on the matter has convinced her that Alan had been holding the gear for someone else. Not, indeed, that that was satisfactory in any way whatsoever, but, at least, it wasn't quite as bad as she had initially anticipated. She had decided, eventually, to handle the matter herself rather than draw Brendan into it. Anyway, given that she could call umpteen examples to mind where, in recent times, Brendan had undermined her authority with Alan, there was no telling that he simply would not have done the same again had she told him about it. Thank goodness she hadn't done so. And now, with Brendan gone for the next few days, what better opportunity than to talk it out with Alan?

Sandra looks at her watch. After 6.30 and Alan has not come home yet. She and Naomi have already eaten. Six o'clock they had agreed before Alan and Naomi had headed off this morning. She envisages Brendan perched on a stool in some little country bar, surrounded by a legion of the local cronies and oblivious to anything that might be going on at home. Across from her sits Naomi, glued, as usual, to the infernal 'Home and Away'.

"Six o'clock we said, Naomi, wasn't it?"

"Yes, Mam." The brevity of her answer is more a way of dismissing intrusion than of attending to what it is she has been asked. In fact, if Sandra were to say that the house was on fire, she would more than likely get the same 'Yes, Mam' in reply.

"Where could he be at all? Did he say anything to you, Naomi, about where he was going?"

"Yes, Mam."

Sandra waits some seconds for Naomi to enlighten her, but nothing is forthcoming. Sandra's frustration mounts.

"Well?"

Not even a 'Yes, Mam' this time. Simply silence.

"Well, Naomi?" Still no response.

"Naomi!"

"Oh, Mam, be quiet, will you? I'm trying to watch this."

And that's the straw that breaks the camel's back where Sandra is concerned. Enraged at Naomi's inattention, she sweeps across the room and turns off the television.

"Right, me girlie, you can sit and watch that now if you like, but don't expect me to take any more of that guff from you, do you hear? Do you hear me, Naomi?"

"Aw, Mam!" And, with that, Naomi hops up off the chair and storms out of the room. Then the deliberate stomping of feet on each step of the stairs is followed by a banging of the bedroom door that reverberates throughout the house.

Yet again, loneliness seems to be Sandra's closest companion. The quiet of the kitchen comes haunting her now. She sits for a time, then sleep eventually gets the better of her. In some respects, that can be considered a relief. She sleeps quite heavily, oblivious to the passing of the hours. Eight o'clock, nine o'clock – and later.

It is a noise outside that finally wakens her, or is it something she has been dreaming? She looks around her, almost as though she is in some strange house where she is trying to get her bearings, then raises her arm and rubs her neck. She has a crick in it from sitting awkwardly in the chair. And now she looks at her watch. Her heart jumps. Holy mother of God – 12.45. Naomi immediately comes to her mind. That and the little fracas they had earlier in the night. She stands, makes her way into the hallway and up the stairs, then looks in on Naomi. She is sprawled across the bed, sleeping soundly. To look at her, one would never think that she could possibly say anything but the nicest things to her mother. Sandra thinks of undressing her and putting her properly into bed, then realises that this, more likely than not, will only stir up more trouble between them. Gently, she frees the quilt from under Naomi's body and spreads it over her. Then she leans across her, kisses her lightly on the forehead and tiptoes out of the bedroom.

On the landing, Sandra knocks gently on the door of

Alan's bedroom. No answer. He is fast asleep by now, she
thinks. Carefully, she turns the handle and eases the door
inwards. She moves from light into darkness, to check, as
she often does, that Alan has not left the music system
playing or, more particularly, to ensure that he has not
forgotten to unplug the little electric fire. Her worry, on
both counts, proves unfounded. She switches on the light
and, sure enough, there's not a sign of Alan to be seen. My
God, she thinks, what a great pity Brendan had not been
that little bit more authoritative a few weeks before. That
might have been just the ticket to ensure that this wouldn't
happen.

Downstairs again and Sandra clasps both hands around
a mug of coffee. Christ, 12.55. Where in the name of God
could he be? With Cillian Reynolds, quite likely, she thinks.
The pharmacist's son. Waves of doubt sweep into her mind
– doubt that she had, more or less, managed to dispel in the
last week or so. But now all the apprehension that she had
felt that night in bed some weeks back, when thoughts of
Cillian being a pharmacist's son had weighed so heavily on
her, come flooding back into her mind. She will phone the
Reynolds and see if Alan is there. She is just about to dial
the number when she thinks better of it. Almost one o'clock
– a little late to be phoning anyone, she tells herself.
Anyway, wouldn't she feel a right idiot if it turned out that
Alan wasn't there?

Back in the sitting-room now and every possibility
comes flashing into her mind. Phone Brendan? No, she
quickly decides, better not – not at this stage at any rate.
There's no more to it, she tells herself, than Alan taking
advantage of the fact that his father is away for a few days.
But, by God, Sandra will give him a grilling when he comes
in. No sooner that resolve than the doubt starts to fill her

mind again. She thinks now of how, in the past few weeks, he has begun to hang out with some of the other local teenagers down at the corner of the street; then of the plethora of rumours abounding in the neighbourhood about what is and isn't going on within that group. The most prevalent suggestion is that there are drugs being taken. All of which leads Sandra once again to think of the find under Alan's bed. God forbid that that's what his hanging about down at the corner has been all about. Surely to God they wouldn't be down there at this hour of the night, she thinks. She gets up and makes for the hallway, turning on the outdoor light as she goes. Just as she is opening the front door, it seems to push itself in on her.

Sandra steps back surprised, then comes forward again. She is shocked to find Alan slouched down on the doorstep, as fully out of things as anyone could be. Fear grips her for a second, but she quickly gathers herself together and goes down on her hunkers beside her son. No signs of injury or beating as far as she can see. Neither can she get the smell of drink. Then the fear that it may be something worse, something far more sinister. She rests her fingers on his forehead, places her thumb across his eyelid and draws it back. The redness of his eye and the tight pinpoint contraction of his pupil confirm her worst fears. She feels nauseous, doesn't know whether to shout or cry. She gathers herself again, draws Alan's left arm towards her and eases the sleeve of his sweater up as far as the elbow. And there, the needle marks she feared make this a night that she will never forget.

4

"This is a family problem and it is important that it be accepted and viewed in that light. That has to be taken as a starting point to the process of rehabilitation."

There is no effort whatsoever on Brendan's part to conceal his impatience as he listens to the counsellor. Sandra, on the contrary, has all the signs of seriousness and is very attentive to what Marian Johnson is saying. As for Alan, his demeanour seems much more akin to Brendan's than to the concern Sandra displays.

"It is always an essential ingredient in assisting the user to come off the stuff that there be cooperation between the various parties involved. There is no overnight solution and it is important to realise that," she tells them. "Bear in mind that it is quite possible that Alan may be feeding this habit for the past two or three years, maybe more. Isn't that so, Alan?"

Brendan emits a little grunt when the counsellor says this. It is hard for her to tell whether it is a sign of approval or otherwise. But Sandra knows. Alan himself says nothing, simply contorts his face and looks away. Then Sandra, as though to compensate for the apparent disinterest being shown by the other two, is at pains to impress her own concern and appreciation on the counsellor. She is worried that the devil-may-care attitude of the other two may ultimately render futile the whole notion of having sought counselling.

Devil-may-care attitude is right, thinks Sandra. That in itself is almost as big a part of the problem as Alan's addiction, which had just been confirmed two weeks earlier. They're lucky, really, that what has been advised is a series of counselling sessions rather than the possibility of legal proceedings of one sort or another. And Sandra, in her wisdom, decided to skip the waiting list and make an appointment with a private counsellor. They could be waiting two or three months on the public system – even longer, maybe. But now, given Brendan's inability to accept that his son is a drug addict, Sandra is hoping that this hasn't all been just a case of money down the drain. She finds it incredible that, despite Alan's five days' hospitalisation after the event, Brendan's attitude could be so closed. And, even worse again, Alan is capitalising on his father's attitude and making out that Brendan has it right.

Of course, what Sandra doesn't realise is that Alan has his father by the short and curlies, that Brendan had been no more down the country with his brother when the incident happened than with the man in the moon. What Alan knows, and Sandra doesn't, is that those few days were spent with Amy, Brendan's bit-on-the-side this past two years. It was by chance entirely that Alan had found out about them. In he goes to a night club in Dublin city centre one night a couple of months back and there they were, all lovey-dovey over in a corner, like a couple of silly teenagers. Alan couldn't believe it when he saw them there, but little did he think at the time that he might turn the whole situation around in his favour. And, by God, did he ever make the most of it.

"Oh! Alan … son," says Brendan, almost falling over himself in shock, "what are you doing here?"

"Me, Dad! What am *I* doing here!" And he looked at his father and then, very deliberately, at the dolly-bird blonde hanging on to him. He recognised her straight off – the secretary from his Dad's school. She was a good-looker all right, about twenty-five, he figured. But, Jesus, her and his old man. If anything, she'd be more suitable for him than for his father.

"Oh … er, this is Amy, the secretary from the school, you know. I think you may have met her before. We were … er …"

"Yes, Dad, I know. You were discussing business, right? Yeah! Teaching matters and the likes."

God, who would have believed it? The middle-aged gobshite and the dolly bird, just like you see in the films. But who would ever think that it would happen in one's own family? It was always someone else's old man. But then, talk about capitalising on a situation …

It was only a couple of days later that Brendan came up with a proposition that he hoped would keep things under wraps. Alan had seen enough and was himself already sufficiently wayward that the attraction of the money was too much to turn down. Little did Brendan know, however, that the two hundred and fifty euro a week he agreed to put in Alan's Post Office Savings Account would partly go to feed a drug habit. He'd have to up the number of German grinds he was giving to earn the money, but still, it would mean his secret would be safe. It was simply buying silence as far as Brendan was concerned, not buying something that could ultimately endanger his son's well-being. His own well-being too, if he stopped to think of it, and that of his marriage into the bargain.

"Two or three years, Alan. Isn't that so?" repeats the counsellor.

"Two or three years! Never. I only took it a couple of times, for Christ sake," says Alan in response. "Jesus, you'd think from the way you're going on about it that I was hooked or something."

"It's quite common for the user to reject counselling. Essentially, it is a denial of the habit. Indeed, sometimes you'll even get a parent who may go into denial also," Marian Johnson says. "I'm always inclined to think that that in itself is some form of self-protection."

An alertness now in Brendan's eyes. He is stung a little by this last comment. The counsellor can discern his discomfort but, in her own mind, she puts it down to her being too direct.

"What I mean is that it can be extremely difficult for someone to acknowledge that a family member could possibly have a problem of that sort, especially where heroin is concerned," she adds. She is silent then, affording them an opportunity – particularly Brendan – to see that there was nothing malicious intended by her earlier comments. But Brendan is his heedless self again and neither he nor Sandra say anything.

"And the element of manipulation, of course," resumes the counsellor, "especially where the user is concerned." Now it is mainly Alan who shows signs of being ill at ease, though Brendan also looks a little flustered.

"Manipulation? What would you mean by that in a case like this?" Sandra asks.

The counsellor looks at Sandra, then shifts her gaze to Alan and then to Brendan. Their discomfort now is very obvious. Then she turns to Sandra again.

"Well, I am not suggesting that it is a factor in this case – that is to say, in Alan's case – but manipulation is often one of the prime strategies of the user in perpetuating his habit. It is a type of playing on the sensitivities of those around him, particularly where other family members are concerned." She glances again now at Alan, then at Brendan, and somehow senses that it is wiser to wind up the session.

"But, I think, that's best left for the next meeting, okay," she says.

Sandra looks towards Brendan and is trying to gauge his reaction to all of this. She can see the stubbornness in his face. Though she realises the extent to which the counsellor is exercising tact in her deliberations, it is obvious to Sandra that Brendan isn't buying any of what the woman has been saying. She is relieved to hear Marian Johnson draw the session to a close and an arrangement is made for next week.

* * *

Silence. Nothing but silence since leaving the counsellor's office over ten minutes earlier. Not one single syllable from any of them. The redness of the traffic light reflects itself across the windscreen of the car and casts mysterious shadows onto their faces, distorting their features. Sandra is fuming with Brendan. Yet again, he has given her no support. And there is Alan, sitting smugly on the back seat, gloating at how things went in the counselling session. Unexpectedly, it is Brendan who breaks the silence.

"Anyhow, as you said, Alan, you only had a couple of gos at it. Isn't that right, son?"

Sandra cannot believe she is hearing this.

"Yeah, Dad, two or three times at the most, I'd say. Certainly no more than four."

Sandra can sense the lie in everything he says. That's bad enough, but now, on top of that, Brendan is there parading himself as the ultimate gobshite, making one stupid utterance after another. She tightens her mouth and re-affirms herself in her resolve not to contribute anything to this stupidity.

"There you are, then, and that's an end to it, isn't that right, son?"

No response from Alan this time. Brendan looks in the rear-view mirror and his and Alan's eyes fix on one another. The threat, the deceitfulness, the secrecy. And Sandra can feel the darkness of the night conspire with Alan's silence to conceal the dishonesty of the situation. She is increasingly hard-put to keep her silence. All she can see now in her mind's eye are the needle marks in the veins of Alan's arm.

"Sure, when you think back, Sandra, to when we were that age, we were all trying that stuff at the time."

Sandra is fit to be tied as she listens to her husband. She cannot decide whether he is more naive than he is stupid.

"Sure, God, there's hardly anyone of our generation who didn't try a little bit of marijuana or a –"

"Oh, shut it, Brendan. For Christ's sake, just shut it. I never heard such stupidity in all my life. Anyway, we're not talking about marijuana or any other soft drug in this case. And what's more, me boyo," she says now, swinging back towards Alan, "we're talking a hell of a lot more than the two or three times that you've been going on about, aren't we?"

Brendan is rocked back by the vehemence of Sandra's attack. He looks into the mirror and, once again, his and Alan's eyes meet. Then Brendan puts his foot down harder on the accelerator.

5

The weeks pass quickly and, in no time at all, it is within six days of Christmas. The family has been finished with the counselling sessions for almost a fortnight at this stage. Or, perhaps, it is more correct to say that Sandra has finished with the counselling sessions because, as far as Brendan and Alan are concerned, they have, most often, absented themselves from the sessions.

"That's a regular pattern with users," the counsellor told Sandra one night. But, despite their non-attendance, Sandra still finds some consolation in the fact that Alan has remained clean of heroin since the night of the fiasco when she found him lying on the doorstep. Of course, since then, he has been prescribed Methadone to keep him off heroin. Sandra is all too well aware that there are those who believe that Methadone is every bit as habit-forming as Smack itself, but it does at least, ensure that he has to attend his doctor once a week to have his prescription renewed. That restricts him to some extent at any rate, Sandra thinks. It is also a help now that he has been back at school since two weeks before Christmas. That can only be a plus in terms of giving some stability and regularity to things.

Sandra has just sat down to a cup of coffee in the kitchen when she hears the sound of a bike being rested against the gable end. She doesn't know whether it is Naomi or Alan. A glance up at the electric clock: 4.10pm. They both had the term's final exams this afternoon – English for Naomi, Biology for Alan. He had ranted on at breakfast time about the stupidity of the system, how it was a schooling rather than an educational system and that exams do little more than assess one's ability to 'absorb all that insignificant bullshit', then spew it all back out again when it is demanded. Sandra and Brendan bit their tongues and let him go on about it. Indeed, if all he was to do was to actually regurgitate the so-called insignificant bullshit, they would be more than happy, given everything that has gone on in recent times.

The opening and closing of the front door happens so quickly that one would be hard-put to say which came first. Then follows a bounding up the stairs. Sandra knows immediately which of them it is. She comes out into the hallway and stands at the bottom of the stairs. Deep down she feels like rebuking Alan for not having come into the kitchen to say hello, but she checks herself in time. She has been learning recently how to let certain little things go unchallenged, thanks mainly to the counsellor's help.

"Don't expect too much of him in the early stages," she had advised. "Even the smallest things can be very difficult for the user when he's trying to stay off the stuff, even more difficult at times than when he's on it."

Still, thinks Sandra, a simple hello surely isn't too much to expect.

"Is that you, Alan?"

A trundling of feet overhead, then Alan comes out onto the landing, buttoning his shirt.

"Yes, Mam."

Sandra notices the fresh shirt immediately. It is his purple silk shirt, the one he wears when he goes dancing. She decides not to make any reference to it.

"I was just having a cup of coffee. Would you like to join me?"

"Sorry, Mam. Have to meet someone in the city centre. End of the exams and all that."

The details of what he is saying are filing themselves in Sandra's mind: someone, the city centre, and all that. That 'and all that' is a regular one of his when he is trying to cover something up. Again the counsellor's advice comes to Sandra's mind. "Yes, and watch for terms like 'whatever it is', 'you know yourself' and 'and all that' – terms that are nebulous, indefinite, non-committal – the user favours them a lot. Very often, they are ways of covering things up; signs, perhaps, that he is not being upfront."

"But what about your dinner? I have it in the oven for you."

"Sorry, Mam. Have to be there by half five."

He moves off the landing and back to his bedroom. Sandra remains standing at the bottom of the stairs, hard-put not to lose her temper. She clenches her fists, sighs a little and walks back down the hallway to the kitchen.

She is seated at the kitchen table now, but her interest in coffee has waned. Her mind is filled with questions once again. Where in the city centre is he going? What's he going in there for? Who has he arranged to meet? Then the questions are shuffled into disarray within her mind when she hears him coming back down the stairs.

"Alan," she says sharply, fearing that he might just head on out the door without so much as a goodbye. She hears him sigh loudly out in the hallway and realises that what she had suspected is exactly what he had intended to do.

"Come in a second before you go, will you?"

Alan takes his time making for the kitchen and, indeed, when he reaches the doorway, he simply leans up against the jamb and doesn't really enter the room.

"Ah, Mam, come on. It's half four already."

"Twenty-five past, Alan, twenty-five past. Now, where exactly is it you are going?" Her tone is firm.

"I told you, the city centre."

"Where in the city centre? It's quite a big place, you know."

"Some dance hall."

"A dance hall. Before teatime? Which dance hall?"

"Well, a dance hall later on in the night. I'm meeting a friend first."

"Who's the friend?"

"Ah, Mam, you'd think I was –"

"Which friend, Alan?"

"Cillian."

"Cillian! Cillian Reynolds?"

"Yeah, yeah, Cillian-bleedin'-Reynolds. Look, Mam, I'm seventeen years of age. I'm not a ch–"

"Exactly, Alan. You're seventeen years of age, not eighteen – not yet at any rate. And you should bear in mind that your Dad and I are answerable for you until such time as you are eighteen years of age."

"Aw, Mam, what sort of friggin' bullshit is this?"

Sandra surges forward, draws back her open hand and slaps Alan a rasper across the face. He is caught offguard and really doesn't know for several seconds what has hit him.

"Don't you dare use language like that to me in this house again or it will be a sight more than a few simple questions you'll have to answer."

Alan is holding his hand to his face now and his eyes are filled with a mixture of defiance and vengeance.

"Well, fuck this for a game of cowboys and indians," he says, staring challengingly into Sandra's eyes, then turns and storms out the front door. The slamming of the door resounds from wall to wall.

Sandra slumps down on the kitchen chair and wraps her hands around the coffee mug. The coffee is cold now, undrinkable. She feels so alone in this whole difficulty;

not one shred of support from any quarter from day one. And as for Brendan – huh – the one whose support she might reasonably expect: he, above all others, has proven to be the least supportive. One would nearly think that, rather than being helpful where Alan's difficulty is concerned, he is intent on adding to the woes. What, in the name of God, is he thinking of at all?

Sandra knows that things between herself and Brendan have not been right this past couple of years. She can remember when she first noticed a change in him. Yes, it was a little over two years ago – two years last August to be precise. A sudden change, it seemed, coming shortly after one of his visits to his brother in the Midlands. One day, he had been his usual self, then, inexplicably, he had become abrupt, disinterested in doing anything with her. All the habits they had nurtured over the years – going to the cinema or the theatre, or even the occasional drink out on a Saturday night – suddenly were things of the past. But worst of all was that they no longer had any physical relationship. That's what Sandra found worst anyhow. That need she had to be held and kissed and told that she was beautiful had gone ignored too. So long a time without that reassurance.

"It's his age, Sandy," her sister Jennifer had told her. Jennifer had just returned from living in the States at the time. Sandra suspected and, indeed, continues to suspect that it may have been pure inability to interest herself in her younger sister's dilemma that prompted Jennifer to say this; just a simple way of passing comment on the situation and having done with it. Jennifer, of course, had had her own problems to contend with and may simply have lacked the energy to deal with Sandra's. Just eighteen months earlier, her husband Bob and she had lost their only

child, Robert Jnr., in a road accident in Connecticut and
they had recently made their move back to Dublin in the
hope that, somehow, it might help alleviate their grief.
"It happens to all men," Jennifer assured her, "but just wait
a while, Sandy, and he'll be smothering you with attention
again, I'm telling you."

Some wait, some while. Sandra knows she's lucky that
she hasn't been holding her breath for any change for the
better. If anything, things had got worse.

The sound of the phone startles her. She raises the
receiver tremulously. "Hello."

"Hello, Sandra."

"Brendan! I was just thinking of you, love." The word is
only out of her mouth when she thinks of how long it must
be since she has called him 'love'. Nearly as long, she thinks,
as it is since he used any term of affection towards her.

"Listen, Sandra, there's a few of us here having a
Christmas drink – end of term and all that, you know
yourself. So, I'm going to be a bit late home."

It is the 'and all that' and 'you know yourself' that
registers with her much more than his message. Just like
Alan. My God, she thinks, maybe I'm becoming paranoid
about everything.

"Fine, Brendan. Who's in the company?"

"Oh, just of a few of the staff members, you know
yourself. Billy and Mike and Joe and three or four others."

Sandra is relieved a little to hear Joe's name mentioned.
He is a steady sort and, if Brendan was at all inclined to go
a little overboard on the drink, she knows that Joe would
see that he was alright.

"Okay, so. I'll leave your dinner in the oven until you
come."

"Well … no … better not to, just in case, you know. This
could go on for a few hours, at least. You never know with

these things. I mean, you know what these occasions can be like yourself. Anyway, can't I bung it into the microwave?" All this is said in a jittery, hesitant fashion.

Sandra is disappointed. Despite communication between them being at a low ebb, she had somehow been looking forward to seeing him, particularly in the wake of the contretemps between herself and Alan. There is silence for several seconds.

"Everything okay there, Sandra?"

"Oh, fine."

"All right, so. Well, listen then, I'll see you later, okay? Or I might even stay in Joe's. But don't stay up for me."

It was a wonder that Sandra managed to hear the final 'me' because there could hardly have been a millisecond between it and the phone being hung up.

"I won't," she says, despite knowing that he is no longer at the other end of the line.

She leans against the jamb of the kitchen door. The receiver is still in her hand and the tears are mounting in her eyes when Naomi comes in the front door.

"Hi, Mam," she says exuberantly, even before she has closed the door. Sandra replaces the receiver and presses herself hard against the kitchen wall. She senses emotion welling up within her, a feeling of forlornness, dejection – loneliness.

"Oh, Mam, you wouldn't believe how easy the afternoon English paper was. An absolute piece of cake. Yeats came up and ..." Naomi prattles on as she walks toward the kitchen, then stops suddenly when she sees her mother so obviously distraught. "Mam, what is it? What's wrong?"

Sandra is incapable of speaking. The intensity of her effort to hold back the tears seems to distort her features. Naomi puts her arms around her. Sandra rests her head on her daughter's shoulder and gives way to her tears.

6

City centre, 1.30am. The lower floor of the dance hall is packed with teenagers. It has been the last day of exams in most of the city and suburban schools and all and sundry seem to have made for the rave in Mad Benny's. The music is pumping, reverberating throughout the building, and the multicoloured rotating lights catch the movement of the young dancers as they bob to the beat. They dance in small, tight groups rather than in couples. Little beads of sweat stand out on their foreheads, glistening when the light catches them. The youngsters exude delight, revelling in the freedom that the end of term offers. Bouncers dot the hall, their spivvy black suits distinguishing them from the dancers. To those who know no better, there seems little need for bouncers to be in attendance at all.

Two young men sit at a table on the balcony above, observing each and every move that is made below. Their watching is punctuated with conversation from time to time. It is mainly the girls they observe.

"See the skirt in the navy blue halterneck," says Cillian, nodding towards a tall, blonde girl who is standing near one of the exit doors. "How about her, then, Alan baby? What do you think?"

Alan shifts his gaze. The sound he makes is a strange mixture of sigh and grunt, but there is no mistaking what he is implying.

"Yeah, man. Yeah, yeah, yeah – that's what I think. Christ, who is she? Do you know her?"

"I knew you'd like her, Alan, my man. That, believe it or not, is the sister of one Johnny Hellerman."

"Johnny the Fix! The owner of the gaff! You're kidding. But she's a f–"

"Yeah, yeah, I know what you're going to say. He's such an ugly fucking mug and she's such a looker. That's everyone's reaction when they hear it. Hard to believe they're brother and sister, isn't it? Still, if he didn't have the marks of that Slish-Slash all over his kisser, he probably wouldn't look so bad."

Alan is not that well up on the Slish-Slash story. All he knows is what he has picked up on the periphery of conversations. He has gathered that it is a form of punishment where criss-cross lines are cut into the flesh with a finely pointed knife. If you're lucky, you get it on the back or on the chest. If not, you get what Johnny the Fix got a good few years back – the full head-to-toe job.

"Jaysus, she's a fucking stunner."

"Hey hey now, Alan, easy on, boy. I've been doing a line with her this past three –"

Cillian stops mid-sentence when he sees a shadow creep across the table. He and Alan look up at the same time and are dazzled by the spotlight on the ceiling to one side of a young man's head. Cillian gestures with his hand and the stranger moves slightly, easing the discomfort for the other two.

"Yes, my friend, what can I do you for?" asks Cillian.

"E, man. What's the twist?" the stranger asks in a whisper.

"Eight a go, man. Five if you want shit. Two clean ones for fourteen – guaranteed." Cillian rattles it off like it's first nature to him. A couple of seconds' silence while the young man ponders his options. He shifts his head momentarily and again the overhead spotlight almost blinds the other two. Then, when Alan gets a proper look at him again, he recognises him as one of Johnny the Fix's marks.

"Twelve the double," the stranger says.

"Thirteen," says Cillian.

A nod and the deal is done. It is over in a matter of seconds. Alan can hardly believe how quickly the interchange is carried out.

"What's the story on doing a bit of dealing?" asks Cillian.

"Naw, no go, man. I'm on Johnny's books, you know."

"Suit yourself. You could freeload in here, man. Have your own gear thrown in and all." Cillian winks at Alan as the other guy ponders the offer.

"Well, how about it?" asks Cillian.

"Naw, I don't think so."

"Whatever you say, my friend. Still, this is hot stuff, man – the best. Anyway, it's down to yourself."

"Naw, I can't, really." There are signs of his resistance breaking now, but he forces himself to get away from the table before he relents. Cillian smirks as he watches him move away and then the smirk breaks into open laughter.

"Christ, Cillian, he's one of Johnny's."

"So what? Fuck Johnny. What the hell do you think brought him over here?"

Alan shrugs and Cillian rests his elbows on the table, then leans in towards him. The music seems louder now, more resonant, and the lights are swivelling at even greater speed than earlier, casting dark and sinister shadows on both their faces.

"I'll tell you what brought him over here. That stuff Johnny's doing is the pits. Any shit of a powder that you could possibly name is in it and no one knows where the fuck it's coming from. And Johnny knows that that's the way it is and so does our buddy who's just been here. They're putting the greatest pigshit into it and just about any junkie who knows his marbles will tell you that."

"Still and all, Cillian, think of the consequences of rocking the boat on Johnny. You know his answer to things. What about his muscle men?"

"Fuck his muscle men. I'm not worried about his or anyone else's heavies. Anyway, there's one thing Johnny understands more than anything else and that's readies, and when he sees the money slowing down, he'll look for another way of making it."

"But that's exactly what I mean, Cillian. He'll send in the heavies and pop go all your plans."

"Spot on, Alan baby, except that what you're not taking into account is that I have a leg in already."

Alan doesn't get his drift, then Cillian nods again in the direction of the blonde below.

"Carole," he says, "she might be a good-looker but she's got more uses than that right now. Unless she's been feeding me shit, it seems that Johnny's looking at the water industry as a possible money spinner at the raves."

"Yeah." It is obvious from Alan's response that he is none the wiser.

"Alan, baby, a little diplomacy, a little bit of back-slapping and arse-licking where Johnny is concerned and, in no time at all, I'll have him believing that the water option is a far better idea than dealing. He won't be long coming to the conclusion that he'd be better off leaving the drug end to someone else – meaning me – and doing the more respectable thing himself, particularly in view of the fact that he owns the gaff. He'll still get his bobs by cutting a percentage on me, but won't have a fraction of the bother he has at the moment. The best of both worlds, as far as I can see."

"Yeah, I know what you're saying, Cillian, but realistically you –"

"Realistically nothing. Listen, Alan, baby, at the moment he's handling stuff that is absolute shit, whether it's E or heroin or crack. You've just seen it for yourself: his own marks coming round to me looking for their gear. Wait until you see, it's not going to take forever for him to figure out what's the sensible thing to do." Cillian bursts into laughter and Alan follows suit.

"I'm telling you, Alan, business will be booming and I'm going to need a good right-hand man to take some of the heat off me, know what I mean? Just keep it in mind, Alan. Think of it, the demand will be wild and we'll be flying. We'll be lucky if we're able to keep up with things without taking a few others in on the action."

They look across at each other, their eyes filled with expectation, smile, then redirect their gazes to the dancers below. The lights are rotating, music pumping and Cillian with a steady finger on it all.

* * *

Soft music fills the bar of The Esquire night club on the other side of the city, where Brendan and Amy snuggle closely. It's nearing three in the morning and, at most, there are only three or four others left in the club. Brendan is fairly well on at this stage, despite their having had a meal beforehand. It certainly hasn't been any desire to dance that has brought them here, simply a need to extend the night's enjoyment and togetherness. It hasn't bothered Brendan that he has lied to Sandra. And yet, he has no desire to hurt her – not at all, in fact. It's simply that the buzz they used to have together is no longer there. Anyway, she'll be well asleep by now, he thinks, oblivious to anything he might or might not do. And, indeed, even if she did know what he was up to, it would be nothing to the fallout that would happen if she knew of his entanglement with Alan. That's when there would be a lot of explaining to be done. He thinks of Alan now. Alan and what he may or may not be doing ...

Mad Benny's and the music is rasping. Alan is seated all alone at the table on the balcony now, looking down at Cillian and Carole dancing below him. In his mind, he is replaying the latter part of his conversation with Cillian a little earlier. "I'm telling you, Alan, baby, my own customers to start with, then Johnny's customers, who'll be automatically mine once he and I have come to an arrangement and, to cap it all, easy access, not just to my old man's stock but to his laboratory as well. Jesus, boy, we have it all sewn up. All you have to do is come in on it with me. Look at it from your own point of view, Alan – all your own gear gratis, no matter what you're doing. What do you say, Alan? Are you in or what?"

"I'll need a while to mull it over, Cillian."

"Well, don't spend too long thinking about it or the chance will be gone. I'm telling you, that pittance your old man is giving you each week won't hold a candle to what you can make out of this. How much are you getting out of him? Four hundred?"

"Two hundred and fifty."

"Two hundred and fifty! Christ, it's hardly worth the effort. Jaysus, I wouldn't raise a sweat for anything less than half a ton. But, I'll tell you this, boy: I can guarantee you ten times that amount per week, minimum. Ponder it, but, as I said, don't take too long about it. I need a right-hand man and, if it's not you, it's going to be someone else."

Alan focuses again on the two below and, as if by

telepathy, Cillian looks up at him. The pharmacist's son winks at his buddy, then raises his right arm and very obviously rubs his thumb against the other fingers of his hand. The message isn't lost on Alan: money. Some thought of his mother is there in the recesses of his mind all the time, but, deep down, he already knows what his decision will be.

* * *

Sandra is restless, turning and twisting in the bed. She turns on her side now and looks at the red neon numbers of the clock-radio yet again: 3.13am. Brendan has not come in yet. Probably in Joe's at this stage, she thinks. He has stayed there a couple of times before in the past year or so – nights when he had gone a bit over the top with the drink.

Now Alan creeps into her mind. She is emotionally exhausted by the anxiety he has caused her. The lack of support she has had to endure hasn't helped her either. She can't remember having heard him come in. Her last memory of consciousness is Naomi coming to the bedside with a mug of hot chocolate. Another look at the clock-radio: 3.15am now and, this time, she notices the empty mug alongside the timepiece. A combination of fatigue and dispiritedness conspire to keep her within the warmth of the covers. Anyway, she thinks, Alan is definitely home by this hour. She turns again in the bed and draws the quilt tightly up around her shoulders.

7

Thursday, 8.30am. The phone in Joe Ryan's is ringing away with no sign of it being answered. Wouldn't you just know it, thinks Sandra. She has spent so long trying to find the number in the directory. Page after page of 'Ryans' and no end of 'Josephs' amongst them. She is in a state of despair since finding out that Alan has not come home. That's bad enough, but a little search in his room has revealed that half the bottle of Methadone which he collected just the day before has already been used up.

She stares at it now, where she left it in the middle of the kitchen table. A litre bottle for two weeks and, though there is really only 700 ml in it, it is alarming that he has taken 350 ml in a day. That's a fair sight more than his prescribed daily dose of 50 ml. Not, now that she thinks of it, that Brendan is going to be much help to her, but there is always the possibility that he might come up trumps some time. Even an understanding ear at this stage might ease the effect of the restless night that she has spent. She is just about to hang up when the phone is answered.

"Hello."

"Hello, Joe. This is Sandra Flynn. I'm sorry to bother you so early on the first day of your school holidays. I hope I haven't got you out of bed."

"Bed, Sandra! Chance would be a fine thing. Not at all. I'm out working in the garage since cock crow. That's what took me so long getting to the phone."

"Well, God knows, this country would be a great place if everyone was as industrious as you, Joe."

"Do you mean that your man hasn't stirred out of the

scratcher yet?"

Sandra is taken aback by the question.

"Brendan?"

"Well, who else, unless, of course, you've finally traded him in for a newer model."

"You mean, he's not there with you?"

"With me?"

"After last night and all."

"Last night, Sandra?"

"Yes, the staff booze-up. Didn't he stay over with you afterwards?"

"Booze-up? I think we have our wires crossed here, Sandra. I was home all night last night. It must have been a few others from the staff were with him. Do you mean he hasn't come home at all?"

Sandra cannot believe she is hearing this. What she doesn't realise is that Joe himself is none the better for the conversation. No sooner has he said what he has said than doubts he's had for some time come to his mind. He has noticed recently that there has been a dalliance going on between Brendan and Amy.

"Well, that's a mystery, Sandra. Maybe he stayed over with one of the other lads. Do you know who was with him?"

"Well, he phoned here and he mentioned you, Joe, and Billy and Mike and one or two others."

"Ah, that explains it, then – he probably stayed with Billy or Mike."

"Yes, maybe that's it," says Sandra, but there is no real conviction in her voice. "That's probably it all right," she adds, trying this time to sound a little more positive. "Sorry to have troubled you, Joe. Happy Christmas."

Sandra sits again, her only companion in the world being

the brown Methadone bottle still in the middle of the kitchen table. 'Physeptone' printed boldly on the bottle's label. It is one of the leading brands, according to the counsellor. Now that she takes more stock of its contents, it seems to her that there is as little as 200 ml left. It was bad enough when she thought there was only 350 in it, but 200! That means 500 ml taken in a single day. Or could it possibly be the case that he is selling the stuff to other addicts? She prays to God that this is not the situation, then tries to banish the suspicion from her mind. But if that notion happens to be right, then things are even worse than she had feared.

The slamming of the car door takes her from her musing. Brendan, thinks Sandra. Thanks be to God. She stands, rushes out into the hall and opens the front door.

"Brendan!" she cries, throwing her arms around him. Her gesture isn't one of any newfound affection for her husband, but she does feel a mixture of relief and support at his having arrived at last. Despite his apparent indifference towards Alan's situation from day one, Brendan's presence is better than being left totally on her own. He stands rigid in her arms, incapable of showing real affection towards her. In a way, the fact that he will not feign affection is some sign of nobility at least, even if the larger picture continues to be one of deceit.

"Thank God you're home. Alan took off for the city centre yesterday afternoon and he hasn't been home since, and I found the bottle of Methadone beside his bed and all that's left in it is –"

Brendan places his hands firmly on her shoulders, ensuring that he has a good hold on her, then pushes her away from him.

"Stop!" he says sharply, and then he shakes her a little. "For the love and honour of God, Sandra, would you ever get a hold of yourself."

Suddenly, she quietens.

"That's more like it. Now, let's keep the cool. Come on in and tell me in a quiet, gathered way." He steers her back towards the kitchen.

She is seated at the table once again and Brendan is fiddling nervously with the lead of the electric kettle. She sobs a little at first, but then composes herself and begins again. This time, the telling is much more collected. She tells everything: her conversation of the previous afternoon with Alan, that he was going into town to meet Cillian and going on from there to a dance in one of the city clubs. Brendan listens attentively, well aware that he himself is caught up in this web of deceit, that he is every bit as dishonest as Alan, if not more so. He is feverishly listening for something that he might latch on to; something that he might somehow turn around to put Sandra at her ease. Mention of Cillian suggests itself as a likely possibility.

"Well, of course, that's it – he's in Cillian's."

Sandra's face lights up and Brendan suddenly feels much more at ease. His nervousness, which derives from the fact that he too has been out all night and a fear that he may be asked to account for himself, has waned somewhat.

"Do you think so?"

"I'd put money on it. That's it, for sure. Teenagers, the last day of the exams, a bit of a tear out on the town, then back to a mate's place to kip down for the night. That's it all right. No doubt about it."

The relief is even more perceptible in Sandra's face. Of course, that's it, she thinks, Brendan is right: he has stayed over in Cillian's.

"God, I feel such a fool," she says. "I'll call Cillian's house." She stands and makes for the hall. "Reynolds,

Reynolds, Reynolds," she chants, as she enthusiastically fingers the list of names in the directory. It is as though the worries of the world have suddenly been lifted from her shoulders. She places her hand across the phone's mouthpiece as she steps from the kitchen into the hall and then turns back towards Brendan. "Why didn't I think of that, Brennie?"

She has unthinkingly called him 'Brennie'. It must be five or six years since last she called him that, maybe even longer. She watches him from the end of the hall as he crosses the kitchen, then disappears from her line of vision. There is something in him now that reminds her of the man she fell in love with over twenty years ago. It seems she has forgotten that he too had not returned home last night. Anyway, that is not the issue; he's been with one of his colleagues. But Alan. Even if it does transpire that he stayed in Cillian's house, he knows all too well that it is a family rule to phone home if anything unforeseen arises. Yet another rule that has gone for a burton since their lives have been discommoded.

There is no answer to the phone in the Reynolds' house. Brendan comes towards Sandra and, as he does, she leaves down the phone and puts her arms around him again. This time, he puts his arms around her and squeezes gently. It is a gesture of pity or, at the very best, one of short-term support.

"Maybe they've all gone off to work already," he suggests. "It's quite probable that Alan is on his way home right now."

"Maybe," she responds, but her tone implies that hope is waning.

"Come on, let's have a cup of coffee." Brendan directs her towards the kitchen yet again. He fills the kettle while she sits back at the table. She's beginning to feel that most of her life is spent sitting at this table, pondering the difficulty that Alan's addiction presents. She raises the brown bottle once again.

"Phy," she says.

"What?"

"Phy. That's what the addicts call it, you know. From what I'm told, they never use the full name for it. Always the short option; the quick-fix attitude in everything, exactly as Marian Johnson told us that first night we went to see her."

Reference to the counsellor makes Brendan a little uneasy, embarrassed. He is well aware of the less-than-full part he played where taking professional advice had been concerned. He comes to the edge of the table, then sits.

"Phy, is it?" He raises the bottle. This is the first time he has even seen it. " 'Physeptone'," he reads and then quietly looks at the details on the label. "Greek, I suppose." The comment is made more to kill the awkwardness than to impart any jewel of wisdom.

"What did you say?"

"Physeptone, Sandra. I'd say it's Greek."

"Greek! Oh, yes, Greek. I suppose it is." And then the thought of how often Brendan's comments – even those made at home – reflect the fact that he is a language teacher makes her smile. To think that was once a trait she used to love about him.

"So, that's the stuff, then?"

"Yes, Brendan, that's it."

"Hmm!"

The click of the kettle switch provides a timely excuse for him to escape the uneasiness of the conversation.

"Tea or coffee?" he asks.

"Hmm!"

"Will you have tea or coffee?"

"Oh, I don't think I'll bother with either after all. I've had more than enough of both in the past few weeks to do me for a lifetime."

Brendan returns to the table and sits down. The ploy to dispel the awkwardness has not worked.

"You should get out a little more in the evenings, Sandra. I notice you have been staying home almost every night right through the winter."

She looks at him. It still amazes her that he can be so totally lacking in understanding of her dilemma. Of course, from day one, he has done so little to try and gain that understanding.

"I just can't bring myself to go out socialising. I feel so ashamed, so worried."

"But listen to me, Sandra – what is there to be ashamed of? It happens in the best of families. Don't you remember the counsellor telling us that?"

Sandra looks at him again. This time, it is more a stare than a look – venomous, berating. She resents that he should even dare invoke anything that the counsellor might ever have said. The cheek of him. It would have served him and everybody else far better if he had only taken her advice a little more seriously at the time, she thinks. But then the thought that, perhaps, his comments are a sign of some newfound caring on his part, of an effort to row in at last with her in handling the situation, prompts her to soften the stare.

"What about Ruth, Sandra? Ruth has always been a good friend. Or Jennifer? Aren't you on great terms with Jennifer?"

How little he understands really, she thinks. It is almost

a year since she has visited her neighbour, Ruth. And to think that they had been such regular visitors to each other at one time. But then Sandra found that she was far more regular in her visits than was Ruth and, anyway, she really hadn't any desire to pour out the sordid details of Alan's problem to her. And that gap in communication which Sandra has felt between herself and Jennifer since her sister's return from the States has never been fully bridged. Despite Sandra's frequent expressions of disappointment, Brendan has obviously remained blinded to that fact.

"After all, she is your sister, and sure that itself is reason enough for you to visit her from time to time. Anyway, it doesn't really matter who it is as long as you have some form of communication with someone."

The utterance has hardly passed his lips when he realises the implication of what he has said. Sandra's stare this time is even more severe. God knows, if ever there was anyone with whom she should be communicating, it should be him. There is tension now, a silence, and resentment mounts in Sandra's mind once more. And, just then, they hear the noise of a key being inserted in the front door. Immediately, their eyes meet.

"There he is now," says Sandra. "By God, he's in for a roasting that he won't forget in a hurry."

"Easy on now, Sandra. That's not going to help the situation any. Quite the opposite in fact, if you stop to think of it. Look, why don't you leave it to me?" and, as he suggests this, he places his hand on Sandra's hand. "Okay?" he asks.

She simply nods her head in agreement. Then Brendan gives her hand a little squeeze, stands and walks towards the hallway.

8

Alan's back is turned to Brendan as he tries to close the hall door without being heard. Brendan stands there watching, wondering what he can say to him that might possibly be heeded. Uppermost in his mind is the knowledge that his own son still has the screws on him and that that, more than anything else, dilutes the strength of any hand he might choose to play. Then, as Alan turns to mount the stairs, he sees his father standing in the hallway. He is slightly taken aback, but quickly gathers himself when he thinks of the hold he has over him. Their eyes meet. There is something sinister in the fastening of their eyes on each other. They both gesture towards the landing at the one time. As Alan begins to mount the stairs, Brendan moves back down the hallway towards the kitchen. He places his shoulder against the jamb of the door and leans his body into the room.

"He's gone up, Sandra. Now, leave this to me," he whispers. "You go on down to Ruth's place for a while or off for a walk, even. It'll do you good to get out in the fresh air."

Sandra has surrendered herself to Brendan's handling of the situation. Somehow, she feels, the burden has been lifted from her. She discerns a major change in Brendan's attitude towards the difficulty, even if it has been a long time coming, and she is heartened by this apparent show of interest. One part of her is cautioning against being overly optimistic while, at the same time, another part is seeing the glimmer of hope still burning. She gathers herself, heads towards the back door of the kitchen and eases her overcoat off the hook.

"That's it, Sandra. That's much better than seeing you sitting there dejected."

He puts his arm across her shoulder and walks her down the hallway to the front door.

Some moments later, as Brendan reaches the landing, he can hear the front gate closing. At least Sandra is out of the way for now, he thinks. He notices Naomi's bedroom door slightly ajar, sticks his head into the room and sees her lying there fast asleep; not a hope in the world that there will be a stir out of her before midday, he reckons. He steps out again, gently draws the door after him and turns to face Alan's room at the other end of the landing. The door is firmly closed already. Brendan can hear the frenetic beat of rap music from within. As he nears the door, he can feel the vibration of the rhythmic beat in the floorboards underfoot. Pumping, pulsating rhythm. He is just about to knock when he pauses. What is he going to say? What can he say, really? It isn't as though he holds the cards in this situation. The reality is that it is he who is at a distinct disadvantage, not Alan. Foremost in his mind is the fear – the danger – that his son might blow everything on him.

He knocks, but the volume of the music ensures that he himself, never mind Alan, doesn't even hear the sound. A second knock and, this time, he turns the handle and eases in the door. The room is in semi-darkness.

The smell of incense is the first thing to greet him, then the sight of a lighted candle by Alan's bedside, throwing dancing shadows onto the ceiling. It takes his senses some seconds to adapt to this unusual mix of light and sound and smell. The first semblance of normality that registers with Brendan is the sight of a little silver spoon on the locker by the bedside. He notices, particularly, how the candlelight is dancing in the wetness of the spoon. A shift to the right and he sees Alan. His son's back is turned to him, as he sits, somewhat hunched, on the edge of the bed, focusing entirely on what he is injecting into his arm. He is oblivious to his father's presence in the room. Brendan comes closer now and, just as he is about to speak, he sees what Alan is up to. Just seeing the needle shocks him, renders him almost speechless. When finally he does say something, it is more involuntary than otherwise.

"Christ!" he mutters, then backs away towards the bedroom door again. Alan jolts upright.

"Dad! What the hell are you doing here?" And, as he speaks, he yanks the needle from the vein and immediately stuffs it underneath the pillow.

"What's that you have there, Alan?" Brendan's voice is trembling as he speaks.

Immediately, Alan spots the nervousness in his father's speech. He himself has been fairly rattled by the intrusion, but he quickly realises that he cannot afford to let his father see that he has put him in any way at a disadvantage. He steels himself, stares hard at Brendan, sinks his hand back in under the pillow and yanks out the syringe with the same vehemence with which he had concealed it. Then, calmly, challengingly, he raises the syringe before Brendan's eyes.

"This? This, Dad? It's called a syringe, you know." Brendan is still visibly shocked, gaping. He cannot believe Alan's defiance and, the more he shows his disbelief, the more brazen his teenage son becomes.

"But then, of course you do. Of course you know that. And inside it, Dad –" he says now, pressing the plunger as he speaks. The sight of the narrow stream of liquid that squirts out from the eye of the needle makes Brendan back away even further. His eyes are big and wide – almost bovine – in amazement.

"That's heroin, Dad! Smack!" The two words hit Brendan one after the other: one-two, almost like the quick hands of a boxer. But, despite the double jolt, he digs deep and quickly decides that he will not let this situation better him. Alan, however, recognises the resolve in his father's eyes and he decides to deal him yet another heavy blow in the hope of taking even the possibility of wind out of Brendan's sails.

"That's it, Dad," he says in a deliberate, challenging fashion, "that's what those two hundred and fifty smackers a week you're banking for me is buying."

This time, Brendan is even more stunned and is feeling less secure in himself than at any point before. Alan is quick to see the effect that this has had on his father and now he decides to go for the jugular.

"You know the two fifty I'm on about, Dad, don't you? You know, the two fifty that you'd prefer me to keep my damn mouth shut about. And we both know why that's the case now, Dad, don't we?"

Brendan shakes his head, as much in disbelief as in answer to his son. The shock of all of this has left him ashen-faced, pole-axed. He comes forward slowly and slumps down onto the side of the bed. It seems as if he's damned if he does and damned if he doesn't.

"Well, Dad, two fifty won't quite do it for me any longer."

Blow after blow after blow, and now this. Brendan cannot believe that a son – his son – would do this to his father.

"This stuff doesn't come cheap, Dad. I think that's something you should realise. That two fifty isn't even pocket money, especially now that I have to use heroin to come down off the E."

Brendan is abhorred, ensnared, but he's all too well

aware that the predicament in which he finds himself is as much the result of his own doing as it is Alan's. He's dreading what may come next.

"Four hundred. That's what I'm going to need from now on and that will only feed half my habit."

"But, Alan, son, think of what you're doing, if not to me then to your mother and yourself, for Christ's sake."

"Four hundred, Dad."

"But Jesus, Alan, I'm already doing extra grinds to make up the two hundred and fifty."

"Four hundred – and that's only for the time being, by the way."

"For the time being?"

"Well, Dad, who knows what I might need a little later on. Habits change, prices go up – you just wouldn't know from day to day. But I think that four hundred is reasonable enough for now, wouldn't you say?"

"Reasonable!"

Reasonable is not the term that comes to Brendan's mind to describe what is being done to him. Deep down, he feels like beating the living daylights out of the little slimeball. But then, that would only exacerbate the situation, he thinks, unless, of course, he was to kill the little fucker altogether. Christ, that's when the shit would really hit the fan. That would be curtains for sure. Brendan holds his head in his hands and looks out through his fingers at the floor. A sigh. A long, weary sigh that presages defeat.

"All right." It is said in the whisper language of the vanquished.

"What's that, Dad?"

They both know that Alan has heard it quite clearly the first time round, but this is the son's way of humiliating the father. Alan knows that if he breaks him fully at this point, his father will be at his beck and call whenever and however he may want in the future.

"All right, I said." Brendan doesn't even have the energy to sound angry at this point.

"Oh, fine, Dad. Whatever you say yourself, so." Alan's sarcasm and cruel, calculated way is shredding Brendan to a nothingness.

"Now, Dad," he says, "be sure and close the door on your way out, like a good man, if that's not too much bother to you."

And now he knows that he has brought his father to heel. Brendan stands. He wants to cry, but some lasting vestige of self-respect enables him to avoid doing so.

Brendan is on the landing now outside Alan's room. It is as if all that had happened there has been a dream. He simply cannot believe what he has been put through in the last few minutes. His own son. But worst of all is that he knows he has brought this misfortune on himself. A sudden increase in the volume of the rap music inside shifts his awareness. He moves along the landing and begins to descend the stairs. Halfway down, he sees Sandra's legs through the clear glass panel as she moves towards the front door. What's she doing back so soon, he wonders? Christ, what's he going to tell her at all? He rushes down the final steps, grabs his overcoat from the stand at the bottom of the stairs and is putting it on as she walks in.

"Sandra, you're back – so soon."

"Oh, my heart isn't in the walk. I'm just so worried by all of this. Where are you off to?"

"Out."

'Out,' she thinks. If a child were to give the same answer, he would be chastised for being smart. Still, better not to make too much of it. Then, raising her eyes towards the landing, she whispers: "How did you get on?"

"Oh, fine, I suppose. Listen, I have to go. I'll tell you about it when I get back. I think it best not to go near him for now – he's gone asleep. See you later, okay?"

"Will you be back for lunch?"

"Lunch?"

"Yes, Brendan, lunch. You're on holidays, remember."

"Oh, yes, that's right. Holidays. Yeah! Look, I'm just dropping over to Joe Ryan's for a while. There's one or two things I'd like to discuss with him." And, with that, Brendan steps outside.

Mention of Joe takes Sandra's mind back to matters of last night.

"Oh, by the way, what happened to you last night? Where did you stay?"

He turns back now. He still has the resilience to summon up a lie. "In Joe's, of course, where else?"

9

Sandra feels listless, a spent force, right over the Christmas period. That brief glimmer of hope, when she had thought Brendan's attitude showed signs of changing for the better, is well and truly gone. New Year's Day and nothing in prospect, as far as she can see; nothing but more downers. Hope had cheated her, lured her in, only to kick her in the teeth again when she found out that Brendan had been unfaithful. Amazing that she hadn't recognised the signs earlier. But then, she thinks, that's the way these things go. She subconsciously convinced herself that Brendan's disinterest in Alan's problem – even his apparent disinterest in her – had something to do with age or with workload or with one of any number of things that might be bothering him. Anything but the true reality. And that reality is hard and cruel and bitter. She could have taken anything better than his infidelity.

Despite it all, however, there is a fortitude which seems to be sustaining her throughout this period of despair. And who would ever have thought that it would be Naomi who would be most instrumental in giving her that fortitude. She has been a jewel since things fell apart just before Christmas. Not that Sandra has told her of the specifics of what is happening – that, she thinks, would be a grossly unfair burden to inflict upon a girl of her age. But, somehow, without anything being said, it seems that Naomi has a surprisingly comprehensive understanding of the difficulties Sandra is going through.

Brendan is seldom seen about the house throughout the festive season. His line has been that he is off playing golf or doing some charitable deed or other. Huh! The very thought of him being off doing a charitable deed would make Sandra laugh if the implications of what he really had been doing were not so serious. And even less again is seen of Alan. He spends the odd night at home but, even then, it always ends in a flare-up between himself and Sandra. He is constantly pestering her for money and coming up with endless reasons as to why she should give it to him. She knows what she would like to give him. This morning again, he tried on the line that he had been pulling almost every morning: "Christ, I have to have money for the bus. I'm meeting my friends in the city centre."

"And where's the thirty euro I gave you yesterday morning, Alan? Are you seriously trying to tell me that that's all spent?"

"Ah, come off it, Mam, get real. Thirty euro! Sure, thirty euro is nothing. I had to go to –"

"You didn't have to go anywhere, Alan. It's possible that you chose to go somewhere or that you planned to do something or other, but don't try to feed me this line about having to do anything."

But Sandra's protestations did not faze him in the slightest. One angle closed, another angle opened: "But I have to go to town, I have to. I have to collect my Phy today."

"Phy! Today? But you're not due another bottle of Methadone for another week. The ninth of January, that's your next due date. You got a double dose last time because of the Christmas and New Year holidays. Take a look at the calendar, Alan. It's marked quite clearly."

"Just thirty euro, Mam, thirty. Christ, you'd think it was a thousand the way you're going on about it. Thirty euro and you'll have it back by the end of the week. I guarantee it."

"Have it back! And where are you going to get thirty euro to give back to me at the end of the week? Anyway, what about the thirty I gave you yesterday? And God only knows how much I've given you before that that I still haven't seen back yet."

"Ah, Mam, come on. I have to go get my Phy. I'm relying on it. You know that."

"I know nothing, Alan. Anyway, how come you need Phy again already if you're only taking 50 ml a day?"

"I lent some of mine to a couple of friends whose stuff had run out and they will be collecting on their prescriptions today. So I'm to meet them in town to collect."

"Friends?"

"Yeah, just friends, that's all."

Sandra looks at him doubtingly. The lies came very readily to him, a trait that had become all too evident to her in recent times. Indeed, he and his father seemed increasingly well-matched.

"So, what's the thirty euro for, then?"

"I told you, Mam – bus money."

"Bus money! For God's sake, Alan, you could go from here to the other end of the country and back again on thirty euro."

"And maybe a game of snooker. You know yourself, Mam."

"No, Alan, I don't know myself. What's more, I don't believe you. Not as much as one single syllable of anything you have said."

Before Alan had so much as half a chance to answer back, Sandra rushed out of the kitchen, up the stairs and into his room where she located the Phy bottle in his bedside locker. Empty. Drained to the last and only half of the prescription period gone. Back down the stairs again, fit to be tied, wielding the empty bottle in her hand. And there before her in the kitchen – her little leather purse wide open in the middle of the table, the back door ajar and neither sight nor light of Alan. She picked up the purse, parted the opening more and saw that every note and coin she had had in it was gone. And that capped what had already been a pretty bad morning for her.

* * *

Sandra and Naomi are seated on the sitting-room settee, an arm across each other's shoulders. Naomi is wearing a dressing gown, its pinkness blending almost perfectly with the colour in her cheeks. Sandra has finally chosen to tell all to her daughter. She is surprised at how soberly Naomi has accepted what she had to tell her. Equally surprising to her is how easy she found it to ring the police, a decision with which – now that it has eventually been made – she feels happy. To think of it, a mother accusing her own son. In one respect, it might well be seen as a surrender of sorts, but, in another, it takes a huge pressure off her and puts the matter squarely in the hands of the authorities. Deep down, Sandra knows that this is by far the better course.

The sound of car brakes outside. "That's them now, Mam," says Naomi.

They jump up off the settee and move over to the window. Already there are two policemen on their way to the front door. Doorbell, answer, and, within a couple of minutes, many of the details are discussed, questions asked, notes taken and the rest.

"You mention Phy. You're talking Methadone, Mrs. Flynn? Are you telling us then that your son is a user?"

"Yes, a user. An addict. He has been on heroin for the

past three years, as far as we have been able to figure out. He's been taking Physeptone under medical prescription since shortly after we found out about the habit, about three months ago. We had contact with your station at the time."

"But are we correct in thinking that you called us here this time in relation to a theft?"

"Yes, that's right." And Sandra proceeds to relate the morning's happenings to the policemen and how, eventually, the money had disappeared from her purse.

"Well, really," says one of the policemen, "I should tell you, for what the advice may be worth, that a theft of this kind would be viewed as an internal matter, if you know what I mean."

"You mean a family matter?"

"Exactly, Mrs. Flynn."

Sandra looks puzzled.

"What I am saying to you, Mrs. Flynn, is that it isn't something, in itself, about which you can do very much. The courts, for instance, would view you as simply wasting their time with such a matter. What about your husband? Is there anyth–?"

The policeman stops in mid-sentence when he sees Sandra turn her eyes towards the ceiling.

"It would be an entirely different matter if your calling us here had to do strictly with your son's addiction," the second policeman says. "As it is, his addiction is secondary here. The emphasis is on the theft. But, let's say, for argument sake, that we were to come upon certain implements or, better still, on drugs in some item of your son's clothing or somewhere in his room."

Sandra's face brightens. Far from being disloyal to her son, she believes that the opposite is very much the case.

She, more than anyone else, realises that it serves nobody well – most particularly Alan – that the urgency of the current situation should go ignored.

"Well, I'm never quite sure what he does or doesn't have in his room these times, despite my efforts to be vigilant, but it was, in fact, the finding of a sachet of heroin along with a number of implements a few months ago that first alerted me to the fact that he was feeding a habit."

The policemen look over at each other when they hear this.

"You're more than welcome to rummage in the room yourselves. To tell you the truth, I would be delighted if you did so," Sandra adds.

Again the policemen look at each other. Now that Sandra has finally taken the step of calling them to the house, she is fully intent on not passing up the opportunity of having the matter resolved once and for all.

"It's the back room, the one beside the bathroom. It's straight in front of you at the top of the stairs."

"Well, Mrs. Flynn, it isn't quite that easy," one of the policemen says. "You see, without a warrant, we have no authority to effect a search."

Several seconds of silence. Sandra is visibly disappointed at the possibility of the chance being missed.

"But," the second policeman volunteers, "if, unofficially, it were to transpire that we accidentally, so to speak, were to come upon an illicit substance, that would certainly constitute sufficient grounds for us to seek a search warrant."

Now Sandra looks confused.

"You know," the policeman continues, "if, just by chance, I were to see something in the bedroom as I passed by the door coming from the bathroom, and if I were to feel a little suspicious about that something, well, there might just be a need to look into the matter a little more deeply."

Sandra's look of confusion suddenly turns to one of understanding.

"Oh, yes. Yes, I understand what you're saying now. Well, do you, by any chance, need to visit the bathroom?"

"Well, it's very nice of you to ask, Mrs. Flynn. Yes, indeed, I think I do." And, with that, the policeman stands, makes his way into the hall and, from there, begins to mount the stairs. Sandra, Naomi and the remaining policeman sit quietly, waiting for a reaction from the man above.

"Mike, can you come up here a second, please?" comes the call within a couple of minutes. The second policeman stands now and follows his companion upstairs. Sandra and Naomi go to the bottom of the stairs. Half a minute later, both policemen walk out onto the landing. They look down at the mother and daughter who are eagerly looking up at them.

"I have reason to believe, Mrs. Flynn, that we have come on an illegal substance in the back room of this house. I regret to inform you that it is our intention to apply to the court to seek a search warrant so that we may conduct a comprehensive search of the room in question."

The policeman who has notified Sandra of his intention grins broadly and so, too, does Sandra.

"Thank God," she says.

10

The day of the court case. Both Sandra and Brendan are there. A vacant seat between them. One of the two policemen is in attendance also – the one who signed the State's case against Alan. And, of course, Alan and his solicitor.

Sandra is shocked when she sees Alan enter the courtroom. She feels the tears well up at first, but then, very deliberately decides to stifle them. It is the first time that she has seen him since the day the police searched the house, some five months before. Since then, as far as Sandra knows, he has been living with friends somewhere in the city centre. School has gone by the board and, since around the time of the theft of the money, he has been drawing some form of an allowance from the State. He looks very grey in the face, she thinks; lost a stone in weight, maybe even two, she figures. His eyes are sunken in his head and his appearance is made even worse by the big black circles that surround them. All the signs suggest that he has gone downhill rapidly.

Sandra is inclined to say something to Brendan about their son's appearance, but she checks herself. Other than the occasional phone call concerning maintenance money, they have had no contact with each other since the beginning of the year. They have been parted since New Year's Day, the day when learning of Brendan's infidelity seemed to bring the whole world crashing down on Sandra. Two huge setbacks almost simultaneously. Thank God, at least, they had the sense to come to a mutual agreement on maintenance, rather than going the legal route and lining solicitors' pockets for doing what they were able to manage for themselves. All of which left Brendan permanently with Amy, while Sandra and Naomi were together in the family home.

But it is an ill-wind, indeed, that doesn't blow some good. Sandra finally finding out about Amy means, at least, that an end has come to Alan's extortion of money from Brendan. That had been a sinister development from the start and, if nothing else, it is good that it is over with. Better still, notwithstanding her obvious concern for her son, is the relief and comparative ease of mind which Sandra is feeling. She and Naomi have grown closer than ever and though Naomi, of course, misses her Dad and Alan, she too is getting on with life in as positive a way as possible.

The judge bears all the signs of austerity. In her early to mid-fifties by the look of her, her appearance made even more severe by her black horn-rimmed glasses. She spends some time scrutinising the documents on her bench, then invites the Prosecution to make its case to the court. She listens attentively to the prosecuting attorney, reflects then on the notes that she has taken and proceeds to invite the Defence to make its submission.

"Before the court, Your Honour, we have an innocent young man who, prior to this appearance, has never been accused of any crime, be that against a person or the State."

No sooner has she opened her mouth than it becomes glaringly obvious that Alan's attorney is a gifted orator. A fine opening with strong and confident delivery, much more impressive than the opening made by the Prosecution. She continues.

"If any misfortune is to be levelled at Alan Flynn, Your Honour – and the Court will note that I very deliberately use the term 'misfortune', not 'crime' – it is that he has the misfortune to be a drug abuser, that he has the misfortune of finding himself in the vicious clutches of heroin addiction and, Your Honour, that, for the past five months, it is also his misfortune to be homeless."

'Homeless' – Sandra is taken aback when she hears the word. Homeless only by his own choice, if really he can be deemed homeless at all. She resents the Defence attorney even using the term and knows that she has done so for emotive effect. But the attorney's skills, her turn of phrase, her ability to pace and reiterate the salient elements in her short delivery have sunk home with all in attendance, most particularly with the judge.

The Defence attorney calmly scans the courtroom, then turns to face the judge again. It is obvious to her that she has already gone a long way towards winning the sympathy of the judge.

"Is it," she asks, "to be a function of this court that punishment be meted out to an unfortunate who, in his short young life has had nothing dealt him by this society but punishment after punishment? That a young man who has never previously offended should be further so ill-treated? That a young man whose misfortune it is to suffer a cruel addiction should be so dismissed? That a young man without abode should now be given the least appropriate shelter of all? Surely not, ladies and gentlemen. Surely not, Your Honour." Her pumping style and the rhythmic repetition of all the emotive words, are, she knows, having the required effect.

"A young man, Your Honour, ladies and gentlemen, who –"

"Objection, Your Honour," the Prosecution interjects.

"On what grounds, sir?" asks the judge.

"On the grounds that the ladies and gentlemen of the gallery have absolutely no judicial function in this matter and it is unfair of the Defence to appeal to them in this way."

"Your Honour," retorts the Defence, "the ladies and gentlemen present are members of the public, are seated in the public gallery of this courtroom and, as befits their status when in attendance at a public courthouse, are as entitled to be addressed as is any other person here present."

The judge nods in agreement. "Objection overruled," she declares. "The Defence may proceed, but in future, when addressing members of the public, you will please make specific reference to them as ladies and gentlemen of the gallery."

The Defence attorney smiles wryly. It is a smile of victory and smugness. "Certainly, Your Honour." Then she resumes the point she had been about to make. "A young man, Your Honour, ladies and gentlemen of the gallery, who, despite every misfortune that has befallen him, has shown the manliness and the fortitude to address his problems in an honest and mature effort to get his life in order."

There is a general stir in the courtroom now. The judge removes her spectacles and leans forward on the bench, apparently eager to hear what is to come.

"Not only, ladies and gentlemen of the gallery, has Alan Flynn had the courage to acknowledge his own addiction, but he has also, of his own volition – and I emphasise, of his own volition – submitted himself for a programme of detoxification in the Central Drugs Rehabilitation Unit, a commitment on his part which is attested to by this document which I now submit as evidence to this court." And, as she announces this last point, she raises a green-coloured sheet for all to see. She then proceeds to the judge's bench and hands her the document. And now there is a silence for some moments while the judge peruses the submission.

"Continue, please," instructs the judge. There is something in the judge's tone that seems to suggest an empathy with the case the Defence is making.

"Thank you, Your Honour," the Defence replies and, for just a moment, her and the judge's eyes hold their stare. Then she turns again to address the general body of the court. "Are we, we who, in our own lives, have not had to endure even the smallest percentage of the troubles with which this young man has had to contend – a young man who has done and continues to do his utmost to get his life back together again – are we going to see this young man go down in this courtroom today? Are we so insensitive to his plight that we are prepared to sentence him to a term of imprisonment and, in so doing, will there be even the slightest shred of satisfaction in our knowing that we have deprived him of that opportunity which now presents itself for him to rid himself, once and for all, of the ugly habit which has been so ruinous to him?"

Her eloquence is masterful. She stops and looks around the courtroom once again. It is obvious to her that they are hanging on her every word.

"Your Honour, ladies and gentlemen of the gallery, all I ask of this court is that it be understanding, that it be charitable and sympathetic towards this young man in the dilemma in which he finds himself. He is a man who has already displayed courage way beyond that which one might reasonably expect of one so young. I ask this court to firmly reject the case presented by the Prosecution against my client and request that Alan Flynn be afforded the opportunity to continue with his rehabilitation."

And, finally, she sits. Silence. Many in the courtroom –
Brendan and Sandra included – feel inclined to stand and
applaud her presentation. Her eloquence has been so
impressive, has so deluded her listeners that many have
lost sight of the reality of the situation. But, despite the
strength of the case presented by the Defence, Sandra has
not lost all of her objectivity. The spectre of doubt and the
seeds of dissatisfaction still linger with her. Thank God she
hasn't brought Naomi to the court with her, she thinks. She
would find all of this particularly hard to take and God
only knows what it could do to her ease of mind with the
upcoming summer exams.

For several minutes there is the buzz of whispering about
the courtroom while the judge considers the presentations
that have been made. Sandra sits in silence, watching the
reactions of those around her. The Defence attorney and
Alan are heavily engaged in conversation and look quite
content with the way the case is going. The Prosecutor,
with one arm stretched along the railing which separates
the area of proceedings from the public gallery, is chatting
with the policeman who presented evidence for the State.

"Silence. Silence, please." The request of the court clerk
is immediately heeded. The judge sits forward now, resting
her elbows on the bench.

"In many respects, the case of the young man before this
court today is a tragic one. It is a case which presents
considerable difficulty for me in knowing for sure what
constitutes the best decision."

As of yet, there is no hint of what her decision may be
and her preamble only serves to heighten the expectations
of all concerned.

"I would like, prior to announcing my decision, to
congratulate both the Prosecution and the Defence on the

excellence, the succinctness and the attention to detail evidenced in their respective presentations. Without that, I very much suspect that this decision, which, as I have said, is difficult, would be even more so. Thank you both."

The attorneys look across at each other, both quite obviously satisfied with the praise given.

"Alan Flynn," continues the judge, "has been accused before this court of being in possession of an illegal substance, namely heroin, in his parents' house on the second of January this year. Of course, insofar as the Defence has readily acknowledged such to have been the case, the burden of proof has been totally removed, and for that this Court is grateful."

Both the Defence attorney and Alan smile on hearing this. The Prosecutor, on the other hand, looks quite apprehensive about what may be to come.

"It is, however, quite obvious from the evidence presented to this court by the Defence that the young man in question is making trenchant and trojan efforts to – if I may borrow from the vernacular – kick the habit." The judge emits a little giggle on her citing of the vernacular, as she has termed it. It is the type of laughter one might easily associate with the notion of being daring in a stuffy setting. Now both attorneys laugh and the infection quickly spreads itself throughout the public gallery.

"I feel, were I to pass down a term of imprisonment on Alan Flynn, that this court would be failing – and failing badly – to show regard for the effort the defendant has made and that, in the long term, the only result of such a decision would be to occasion a regression in his rehabilitation."

It is glaringly obvious to Alan now that he has managed to beat the rap.

"In the final analysis, it is the well-being of this society and, indeed, the well-being of the defendant himself which this court is obliged to take into account. And therefore, having considered all facets of the case, while, at the same time remaining cognisant of the fact that, in legal terms, Alan Flynn is past the age of minor, my decision is in favour of the defendant. He will, however, be made a ward of this court for a period of six months from this date, the conditions of which will be explained to the defendant and his legal representative in my chambers after this case has concluded."

Sandra has no memory of anything else being said. Her dominant feeling is one of disappointment. Not that any mother would want to see her son sent to prison – not at all – but, in her heart of hearts, she feels there is a need to make him fully accountable for the seriousness of his actions. She is all too aware of the cleverness of the case presented by the Defence attorney. But then, when all is said and done, isn't that what she's employed to do? Doing her job and doing it most effectively indeed. But Sandra is fearful that the upshot of this decision may be to give Alan the impression that it is possible to twist and turn the law in one's own favour and still remain free to do as one wishes.

* * *

A little later. Brendan and Sandra are seated on a bench in the foyer of the courthouse, that same space between them as before. Small talk from time to time, but even that is more than what either of them might truthfully opt for. Were it not for the fact that they are waiting to see Alan when he comes out of the judge's chambers, they would have gone their respective ways as soon as the proceedings had finished.

"Well, how are things at school?" asks Sandra.

"Oh, getting through it. No shortage of blackguards, too much correction and not half enough time to do the things you want to do – you know how it is."

"Yes, I do." Sandra's response is as caustic as it is terse.

"And yourself, Sandra? And Naomi? Are things okay?"

"Oh, never better, Brendan. Sure, we're flying, flying." This time, the dominant feature of her answer is a sarcasm. Brendan is increasingly ill at ease.

"So, what do you think of this morning's proceedings?" he asks. She looks at him sharply. Deep down she is seething with anger towards him. The cheek of him to ask her that, she thinks.

Still, it will serve no purpose to let fly at him. Things are bad enough without adding to the litany of woes. She is just about to respond when they spot Alan and the Defence attorney enter the foyer. They stand and, for a couple of minutes, look over at their son as he and the attorney converse. Then, a handshake and the attorney re-enters the judge's chambers and Alan turns towards the front door of the building.

Just as Sandra is about to call after Alan, Cillian appears on the scene. He has, apparently, been sitting all the while on one of the benches beyond the portico, at the far end of the foyer.

"Alan, Alan, my man!" says Cillian, and his deep voice echoes resoundingly throughout the high-walled foyer. And, as Alan sees him, he extends his open palms and Cillian slaps his own down on them.

"What did I tell you, man?" says Cillian, and they both burst out laughing.

And Sandra now feels all the more ill at ease and so too, to give him his due, does Brendan. They look at each other. Brendan knows how eager she had been to speak with Alan, but he can see that this unexpected interruption has jarred her somewhat. He will take the initiative on her behalf.

"Alan," he says, projecting his voice across the foyer.

Both Alan and Cillian turn towards him at the same time. When they realise who it is, they simply burst into laughter again, turn and leave the building. Brendan finds himself caught somewhere between amazement and anger at this reaction, but he is even more concerned for Sandra now than for himself. He turns towards her as she, dejectedly, eases herself back down onto the bench.

11

Sandra's mind is in a state of flux since leaving the courthouse. She is still in Brendan's company. She cannot even remember how they selected the pub where they find themselves now. Probably something as simple as it being the one closest to the courthouse. All the more surprising to her is that she has allowed herself to come here with him, given all that has happened in their marriage in recent times. But then, situations such as this are often far from logical. She is a spent force after the morning's proceedings, badly in need of the pot of tea and sandwich which Brendan has gone to the bar to order. She looks at him as he stands there. The memories. Why did all that happened have to happen? He's on his way back from the bar now, a sizeable wooden tray held out in front of him. He lays it on the table and begins to dole out the various items of delf and cutlery. Sandra smiles broadly.

"You haven't changed a bit, so."

"How do you mean?" asks Brendan.

She directs her gaze at the tray and at the various bits and bobs with which he has strewn the table. How often, over the years, they had laughed about how much Brendan detested being waited upon in such places. He always much preferred to take his own order from the bar rather than have some waiter or waitress fussing about him.

"Oh, that. Well, you know what they say about the old dog."

Then they both laugh. Sandra has already poured the tea. Brendan raises the milk jug and passes it to her. As she takes it their fingers touch and, privately, each feels a vestige of that excitement they used to feel. There is a momentary racing of pulses, but neither allows anything to go any further than that. Sandra, a little embarrassed, raises the cup to her mouth.

"Thanks be to God. I'm weak all morning for the want of a sup of tea."

"You can't beat it all right."

What they say is no more than filler-talk but, nonetheless, it serves to dismiss the awkwardness they feel about the accidental contact. Then there is a silence for a time. A chance, perhaps, to contemplate the goings on of the morning or maybe even to ponder the effect that the touch has had on them. Who knows?

"I thought that ..."

"What did you ..."

Strange, after the period of silence, that both should start to speak again at exactly the same time. They burst out laughing.

"Go ahead," says Brendan.

"I was only going to ask you about your impressions of the morning. What did you think about it all?"

Brendan seems cautious, unsure that he should proffer an opinion. He is well aware of how his passing comments on Alan's situation can irritate Sandra and, God knows, he can't exactly blame her for feeling that way. She can see his hesitation and moves to reassure him.

"Go on. I'm not going to bite your head off. To tell you the truth, given how I'm feeling at the moment, I don't think I'd have the energy to get annoyed."

"Well, since you ask, I don't honestly think it was the wisest of judgments to let him off so lightly, even if he has been made a ward of the court."

"My feelings exactly. Simply letting him off to do more

of what he has been at already. He's bad enough as it is, but
God only knows what he may get up to now. I just can't see
any sense or reason to it as a decision."

"Hmm."

"And did you see the state of him, Brendan? He looks
absolutely wretched. God knows, he –"

"Whisht, a second!" Brendan gesticulates in the direction
of the door. In comes Alan and Cillian along with a tall
blonde girl. She is extremely good-looking. They stand in
the middle of the pub, glancing around them, but totally
oblivious to the presence of Sandra and Brendan. Then
they move into the alcove that backs onto the one in which
the estranged parents are seated. There is nothing separating
them from each other now but the wooden, stained-glass
partition between the alcoves. Brendan and Sandra make
all sorts of contortions as they gesticulate to each other to
listen to what's being said on the other side.

"I told you, Alan-boy, that old line about you doing
your damnedest to kick the habit – it gets them in the solar
plexes every time." Cillian is the speaker and the other two
laugh heartily.

"And having a woman on the bench is an added
advantage, I'm telling you, boy. Christ, women are so much
softer than men on these issues," says Cillian.

"Hey, hey, easy on there, boy, watch the sexism. That's
against the law, you know. Equal rights and all that stuff,"
the girl says, and this too is followed by another outburst
of laughter.

"Well, sexism or not, Cillian, it worked to a tee this time,
anyway," says Alan, "and, with all due respect to yourself
and the women of the world, Carole, whatever may be said
about your brother Johnny from time to time, he was spot
on when it came to calling this one. It was a master stroke

advising us to go with a woman solicitor. That really capped it all."

Brendan and Sandra look at each other aghast. They cannot believe that they are hearing this from their own son. Sandra is tempted to jump up and give all three of them a piece of her mind, but Brendan spots her anger and quickly moves to stop her. A simple placing of his hand down on hers is enough to dissuade her.

"Take it easy, Sandra. Let them go a while."

"Would you like to order?" It's the waitress.

"Yeah. Two pints of Bud and a … what are you having to drink, Carole?"

"Carole! Who's Carole?" says Sandra.

"Shush a second 'til we see."

"A G'n T."

"Yeah. Two pints of Bud and a G'n T," says Cillian.

What they have already heard Cillian say gives Brendan and Sandra some insight into the character of the young man their son is hanging around with. It was a mixture of naivety and sheer lack of knowledge of Cillian that had Brendan thinking he was a grand upright young lad. Far from it, it would seem now. When he thinks of it, Brendan can't remember ever having actually met the boy. Even Sandra has only met him three or four times at the most and the last of those must be all of six months ago.

"Well, fair dues to Johnny, he knew his marbles when he advised against going with FLAC. That woman was an absolute peach compared to some of the duds of solicitors you're stuck with on Free Legal Aid."

"You can say that again, Cillian."

"Hush a second, here comes the hard stuff," says Cillian.

The waitress places the drinks before them and then is gone again.

"So, what are the conditions of you being made a ward of court then, Alan?" asks Carole.

The question prompts yet another outburst of laughter from the young men.

"Conditions! God, Carole, I don't think you could even call them that. I have to present myself at the local cop shop once a week, not offend again within the next six months and, other than that, I'm free to do what I want when, where and how I like."

"Shit," says Carole, and then more laughter. "Here's to you, man," and the toast is followed by the sound of glass on glass.

The sudden clinking of the glasses jolts Sandra. Every single question she had had in her mind to ask her son in the foyer of the courthouse has been answered for her now. But what bothers her even more than the nature of what's been said is the downright brazenness of Alan's answers.

"That's as much as saying that you're totally free to keep the hand in on our own little bit of action, then, Alan-boy," says Cillian. "My old man and old lady are off on a month's holidays at the end of this week and that's going to leave the lab at the back of the shop free for the taking. And now that Johnny's on board with the new arrangement, we can make an unmerciful batch of the stuff. Now, boy, are you happy or what that I ever mentioned it to you?"

"Bleedin' right, Cillian, my man."

"Jaysus , you know where you could tell your old lad to stuff his two hundred and fifty miserable smackers now."

"That's for sure," says Alan. "He could shove them up his arse for all that I care now."

And this time the youngsters' laughter is in celebration of the scam they have going.

On the other side of the partition, Brendan's mood has

to do with anything but laughter. He is fit to be tied. His inclination is to jump up and to beat the living daylights out of them, especially Alan. But, this time, it is Sandra who keeps a cool head. It is she now who places her hand on Brendan's.

"Let it go, Brendan," she whispers. "What good is it going to do if you chaw them out of it? They're only going to laugh at you." He nods, knowing she is right. No good in the wide earthly world, he thinks.

"Come on, let's get our arses out of this middle-class shite-hole of a gaff," Cillian says, and there follows the rustle and bustle of their movement.

Brendan immediately turns in towards Sandra, holding his hand against his cheek and leaning an elbow on the table as he does so. The youngsters pass without noticing them. Once gone by, Alan's parents watch the trio heading out the door.

"Well, well, surprise, surprise," says Brendan. "That's the calibre of a boyo our lad has turned out to be. And Cillian! I thought he was supposed to be a fairly respectable young fellow."

"But, sure, that's what I had been trying to ..." Sandra stops herself. Where's the sense, she thinks, in going back over what she had and hadn't done to impress on Brendan what was going on? It's all water under the bridge at this stage, she thinks. No sense in dragging it all back up again.

"What were you going to say, Sandra?"

"Oh, nothing. Nothing whatsoever, Brendan." She raises the teacup, looks out over its gold rim at Brendan and sips from it.

12

Later that night. Mad Benny's is as vibrant a centre of activity as usual. The intensity of heat inside the building has compelled many of the young male dancers to remove their shirts. All the usual patrons are there – the dancers on the lower level and those who frequent the balcony area seated at their habitual spots. There is the regular coming and going from the tables. The occasional person on this upper level may bob about a bit to the rhythm of the music but, in the main, the greater interest is in conversation.

"Just as you called it, Johnny man," says Cillian. "And if you had only seen the judge. She swallowed the whole damn lot, hook, line and sinker." Then, all four seated at the table burst into laughter.

"She! Do you mean to tell me the judge was a fucking woman, Alan-boy?" says Johnny the Fix.

"Yeah, a lady. Sure, we knew we were away with it as soon as we saw it was a skirt," says Alan. "And then, as if things weren't going our way enough already, wasn't my own attorney a woman too."

"What did I tell you the day you came looking for advice, Alan, baby?" says Johnny. "A skirt will always do the trick. Still, it was a huge stroke of luck to get a woman judge as well. Jesus, one of them in a courthouse is worth any ten men. But two women, lads, and you're away in a hack altogether." And then more laughter and not without reason.

"Oh, that's it all right, lads. Leave it to the women of the world. When push comes to shove, they always come up trumps. Leave it to the sisters, boys," says Carole, half-mockingly. The men are silent. They all stare at Carole, feigning anger. They hold their stares and, just as she shows signs of being ill at ease, they burst into laughter again and she realises that they have been trying to put the wind up her.

"Well, fuck you," she says, half-laughing, while, at the same time, faking injury at being put under pressure. Then, before she gives the game away, she gets up and makes for the stairs. The three men watch her as she begins to descend the spiral staircase. As soon as she is out of sight, they crouch in around the table and begin discussing business.

"You were saying something earlier on about there being a problem, Johnny. What's the story?" asks Cillian, and then, before Johnny actually has a chance to answer, Cillian turns to explain to Alan. "You saw Johnny calling me aside when we came in earlier tonight, Alan?"

"Yeah, I noticed that all right."

"Yeah, well, he was telling me that there's a little hiccup in the matter we had been discussing."

"Hiccup?" says Alan.

"Exactly what I said myself, Alan-boy. So then, Johnny, what's the buzz?"

Johnny leans in even more closely. "Well, it's this. You know the Bradys?"

Mention of the name causes Cillian and Alan to look over at the far end of the balcony where the Bradys are seated – three brothers who have pretty much the same type of racket going down in a couple of the other city centre clubs as Cillian and Johnny have going in Mad Benny's.

"Yeah. What about them?" asks Cillian.

"Well, they want a cut of the action," Johnny whispers.

"A cut of the fucking action! Well, they can f–"

"Shh, Cillian, easy on, man! A cut, that's all. It's not as if they're in for a takeover – not at all. A cut, that's all. Nothing more."

Cillian emits a long sigh and then is silent for several seconds. Alan, seated beside him, is taking stock of his two comrades. He is anxious about what may be about to happen, but he himself doesn't have the confidence to make any appreciable contribution to the discussion.

"And just how much exactly is a cut, Johnny?"

Johnny is hesitant.

"Well, Johnny, how much? How much is a fucking cut?"

"A cut, Cillian, a cut. You know yourself –"

Cillian thumps his fist down hard on the table top, catching the other two unawares. He is not to know that the Bradys have now become aware of the tension developing in the Mad Benny ranks.

"No, I don't fucking know myself. Now, how much, Johnny? A quarter? A third?"

Johnny is slow to answer, even more hesitant this time than he had been earlier.

"Half," he says eventually, keeping his eyes fixed firmly on the centre of the table.

There is silence now. Even the throbbing of the music throughout the dance hall does not impinge on their minds. And then Cillian starts laughing. But his laughter is strange, nervous – something distinctly malicious about it.

"Half?" says Cillian gently. "One fucking half of all the action in this joint?" This time he has been more forceful. His eyes fasten on Johnny the Fix and, for several seconds, there is nothing said. Cillian shifts his gaze in the direction of the Bradys, then back again. Then, in a slow measured tone, "Johnny, you can tell them to go fuck themselves."

"But, Cillian –"

"Don't fucking 'but Cillian' me on this one, Johnny. We have a fucking arrangement where this is concerned and now you're trying to do the dirt on me, Johnny."

"Christ, Cillian, no. You're getting me wrong here, man. For fuck's sake, there's plenty going down to do all of us. It isn't as if –"

"Well, fuck you, Johnny. Fuck you. What's the real story here? They have you by the balls for something, is that it? They have you by the balls and this is your way of squaring things up. Is that it, then, Johnny?" Cillian is pointing threateningly at Johnny as he unleashes this barrage.

"Or is it something else, Johnny? Maybe the bastards have promised you more than you're getting out of me. Well, Johnny? A bigger cut for yourself. That's it, isn't it, Johnny?" The speed and anger in Cillian's questions is violent.

"Naw, come on now, Cillian. You've got it all wrong here. You know that I'd never –"

"Don't give me that shit, Johnny. You know right fucking-well what you're about, boy. An eye for the bigger cut, that's what all of this is about, and fuck the rest. Nothing more, nothing less."

"Naw, Cillian, you've got the wrong end of things entirely."

"No no, Johnny, I haven't got the wrong end of things. I've got it right. But you go on ahead, go on. Give up your half of the action, if you want, but don't fucking think for one minute that I'm letting those shitheads, or anyone else, take half of my action from me. Get me, dickhead? Twig?"

Alan is increasingly nervous as he listens to this. Even Johnny is anxious, particularly because the Bradys are so close by.

"Come on, Cillian, man, let's leave it for now, huh! What

do you say? We can discuss it in the office later on," and, as Johnny speaks, he places his hand down on Cillian's. Cillian immediately brushes Johnny's gesture away, gives him a dagger's look, then turns away from him entirely.

Silence now. Alan looks on nervously, afraid of another eruption at any second, though even a temporary abatement is better than what has just been going on.

"Listen, Johnny, you know as well as I do that that stuff the Bradys are doling out is pure shit. It's even worse than that fucking pig swill you were pushing before you let me in to handle distribution." This time, Cillian's speech is calmer, much more reasonable and measured.

"Look, Johnny, they're pushing Skag all over the place and pretending that it's E. And it's full of the worst shit possible – Daz, Omo, fucking rat powder – anything that'll function as a bonding agent for the tablet. You know that, Johnny. And I'll tell you something else – the Smack they're pushing in their own clubs is some of the dirtiest shit that has been doing the rounds in years."

"Come on, Cillian, man, take it easy. You're getting way too hyped up about this. All they're asking us to do is meet them, just so that we can discuss the possibilities."

"Yeah, sure, Johnny. And I'm telling you that there are no fucking possibilities. Right? You, me and Alan here, Johnny, and that's it – just the way we had agreed. Now, you can put a fucking sock in it and forget this shit of talking with the Bradys."

As Alan listens to all that is going on at the table, he cannot but be aware of the major change he has seen in Cillian lately. Only a few months ago, when the notion of Cillian taking over the handling of the stuff from Johnny was being floated, Alan knows that Cillian himself was somewhat apprehensive – fearful of Johnny, really – even if he wasn't prepared to admit that at the time. But now, given how successfully the operation has gone, Cillian's self-confidence is sky high and the notion of confronting Johnny as he is doing doesn't cost him a second thought.

"But, Cillian, it isn't ev–"

"Put a zip on it, for Christ's sake, Johnny. I don't want to hear it. You're trying to play both sides here and still come out a winner. Well, you can fucking-well forget it. I'm not fucking buying in to any double-dealing."

Then, unexpectedly, Cillian jumps up from the table and heads directly towards the Bradys. The three brothers see him coming – and they also see the anxiety on the faces of Johnny and Alan following, trying to stop Cillian from making matters even worse. The Bradys move their chairs out from the table a little and brace themselves for Cillian's arrival.

"What the fuck ..." rants Cillian as he comes towards them. But no sooner has he begun than Ringo, the oldest of the Bradys, unleashes an unmerciful punch into his stomach, stopping him mid-sentence. The other Brady brothers have already grabbed an arm apiece and have forced him over to the railing of the balcony. The combination of the swirling lights and the pain in his stomach has Cillian totally fazed as his head is forced out, face-up, over the balcony. Then Ringo grabs hold of his hair and jerks back his head abruptly.

Despite his view of things being very much inverted, Cillian has no difficulty in recognising the implement which Ringo Brady is holding now – a knife, its blade catching all the strands of the multicoloured light being projected by the mosaic glass sphere hanging from the ceiling of the dance hall. Brady presses the sharpened edge against the flesh of his neck and Cillian does not know whether it is the possibility of being pushed off the balcony or of having his throat slit that scares him most.

"Do you feel that, Cillian, boy, do you?" asks Ringo.

Cillian's eyes are bulging and, try as he might, he is incapable of speaking.

By now Johnny and Alan have reached the scene of the fray, but they are wary of getting too involved. There's always the possibility that the Bradys' attention might shift to them. They stand there, hopelessly looking on.

"Well, Cillian, sonny, I could do whatever I like to you now – do you know that?" says Ringo, and, as he speaks, he presses the blade a little more heavily against the flesh.

Cillian nods the slightest nod, afraid that anything more than that will definitely see him cut. Then, slowly and very deliberately, Ringo scores the flesh with the blade, then cuts. Blood spurts out. The cut is short – three-quarters of an inch, maybe, certainly no more than an inch. But it is more than enough to make Cillian buckle at the knees. The Bradys let go of Cillian and, before he even knows what is happening, Alan is grabbed and slit on the cheek. This slit too is small – just a warning – and now Ringo has grabbed a hold of Johnny. Alan and Cillian, their backs against the balcony railing, have blood streaming from their wounds.

"Get the fucking act together, Johnny, boy, or next time we won't be talking about a few harmless little slits. Know what I mean, do you?" says Ringo.

Johnny's eyes are bulging in their sockets, focused sharply on the point of the knife which Ringo is holding up before him. He nods and, as he does so, he feels Ringo ease his grip on him. Then, without the slightest warning, all three Brady brothers grab the table they had been sitting at and throw it over the balcony railing. On the floor below there is mayhem amongst the dancers – screams and screeches – none of it of any consequence whatsoever to the Bradys.

Ringo Brady grabs hold of Johnny once again. "Remember, Johnny, I want a fucking answer and I want it soon. No more shitehawking, right?" he warns, then lets go of him. "Come on, lads, let's get the fuck out of this kip," he says, and, with that, they're gone.

13

Summer passes into autumn and on into winter. February has come around again and, in the passage of the months, much has happened to ring the changes, particularly where life for Sandra is concerned. She has been working full-time for several months now and most wonderful of all for her is the fact that she has met a man, Matt, whose company she very much enjoys. The thought of her dating someone seems so amusing to her at times. Somehow, that is something, in her mind, that happens only among young people. Nonetheless, there is comfort in the thought – almost as much comfort as she finds in Matt himself.

It is quite some time since she and Brendan have seen each other. There is the occasional contact, but that is always on the phone and, even then, it is only to discuss matters of maintenance or something that relates to Naomi. By now, Sandra has learned to be considerably more civil towards Brendan than she had found possible in the early stages of their separation. Thank God for that at any rate. When all is said and done, where's the sense in being vindictive, she thinks. If anything, it only worsens matters and, in recent times, she has come to realise that. Generally, her outlook on life is more positive by far than has been the case for quite a long time.

All of which contributed, in no small way, to Sandra's composure and calm when first she heard that Amy was expecting Brendan's baby. It would have been nice if Brendan had taken the trouble to lift the phone and tell her the news himself rather than her finding it out through Naomi. But, in some respects, she can understand what a difficult situation that would have been for him. How could he tell her, really? And even if he did, what sort of a reaction might she have had to the news? No, it is better by far that he imparted it to Naomi, full sure that she would pass the news on to her mother. Anyway, when she comes to think of it, didn't she leave it to Naomi to tell Brendan about Matt?

As for Sandra herself, the best thing she had ever done was to go back working outside the home. What, in the name of God, had possessed her all those years back, to pay any heed to Brendan urging her to stay at home after Alan was born?

"Going out to work," said Brendan at the time, "with a small baby at home! God, I don't think that serves any good at all, no matter what your liberals and women's libbers might or might not say. A child needs the constant attention of a mother in the home, especially in the early years."

Mind you, Brendan wasn't exactly rushing to volunteer his services as a childminder. Chance would be a fine thing. All that said, Sandra could not deny that that first year at home with Alan was very pleasing to her; she was still very much under the spell of being a mother for the first time. Even the second year wasn't that bad. But, by the time the third year came around, the bug to go back working in the bank had begun to bite. She was just about to inquire into the possibility when she found herself pregnant with Naomi and that decided the issue for her once and for all. Thereafter, the years just seemed to fly by. But all that is over now. She is still amazed that, after the guts of twenty years of keeping house, she could find it in herself to go out there and look for a job. Even more amazing to her is the fact that, despite all that she has heard, year in, year out, about the lack of opportunity for people of her age, she has actually succeeded in landing a position.

It's almost three months now since she started in the Credit Union and, in that time, nearly all her worries have abated. All but Alan. She has hardly heard a thing of him since that day in court, over six months ago. By now, as far as Sandra knows, he is clear of any hold the court had placed on him. Naomi had said a couple of times that she thought she had seen Alan and Cillian in the distance, but then, she could not be absolutely sure it was him. As it happens, the only time that Brendan had mentioned anything on the phone other than Naomi or matters of maintenance, it was to refer to Alan. He had seen him some two months earlier. He was almost sure that it was Cillian with him. They were outside a night club on the quays, near the city centre. Sandra still remembers how her heart jumped when Brendan told her that.

"And how were things appearance-wise, Brendan?"

Her hope was quickly dashed when Brendan mistook her question to be about the night club. Then, even when he realised his faux pas, he could only report that he had been in his car at the time and, besides, it was night-time and hard to make out how Alan may have looked anyway.

That was the incident which placed Alan back at the forefront of her mind. Not, indeed, that she was either likely or able to dismiss him totally, but she had, quite deliberately, tried to relegate the importance of what had happened into a secondary slot, all in an effort to pick up the strands of her own life once again. And, indeed, why not, she had thought? Particularly in view of the fact that he himself had not been prepared to take responsibility for his actions.

But the news that Brendan had sighted Alan certainly brought the matter up again. It rekindled that old curiosity and, if anything, that curiosity had been growing ever since. She had never had any contact with the Reynolds – Cillian's parents – prior to that, but since the conversation with Brendan, she has made a practice of phoning Cillian's mother once a week, always hoping that she might have news of Alan.

"Well, strange as it may seem, and despite the numerous times that Cillian has spoken about your son, Mrs. Flynn, I have never actually met Alan," said Mrs. Reynolds that first time Sandra spoke with her.

She seemed to be a kind, gentle woman and Sandra never had any reason to think otherwise since the time of their first conversation. It was strange, however, that she should say she had never met Alan. Sandra was certain that Alan had, from time to time, mentioned having met her. Crossed lines somewhere in the equation, thought Sandra, none of which affected her opinion that Mrs. Reynolds was a good sort.

"Oh, our Cillian," said Mrs. Reynolds, when Sandra explained the reason for her call, "he certainly wouldn't have anything to do with drugs or anything like that, apart, of course, from helping his father in the pharmacy from time to time."

"Of course," said Sandra.

"We really don't see him so often now, since he has taken the year off from university. But I do know, from occasional conversations with him, that he and Alan see each other on a regular basis still. So, you can take it from me, Mrs. Flynn, that if your son is in Cillian's company, he can't be up to anything where drugs are concerned. Now that I come to think of it, the last time that Cillian was here – three or four days ago – he mentioned, right enough, that Alan had visited him in his apartment."

"Apartment?" said Sandra, and it was obvious from her tone that she was taken aback on hearing this.

"Yes, Cillian's apartment. Well, of course, it isn't his own apartment. My husband and I thought, given that he would be studying for three or four years, that it would be handy for Cillian to have a base that was somewhat more central, nearer to the university. You know yourself how it can be. So, we decided to buy an apartment in the city centre. Then, when Cillian took the year off, we thought that it would be better for him, in terms of his own independence and all, that he have his own place. It's an investment more than anything else, really, and well worthwhile, given the tax break, of course."

"Of course," replied Sandra again. Her mind was running wild at the thought of all the possibilities a city-centre apartment might offer to the likes of Alan and Cillian.

But there wasn't any sense in getting into a discussion about that with Mrs. Reynolds. What purpose would it serve to tell the woman that Cillian had been along with Alan that day of the court case? Or to mention the nature of their conversation overheard in the pub later that day? No purpose whatsoever, other than to upset the Reynolds' household also. God knows, it was bad enough that one family had already endured such trouble without passing it on to somebody else. Sandra did, however, ask Mrs. Reynolds if she would mind her ringing her from time to time. That, at least, would leave the lines of communication open and, in the event of there being any news of Alan, she would be more likely to hear of it that way. "Certainly, Mrs. Flynn, feel free to phone whenever you wish. Once a week if you like. If nothing else, a little conversation can't do a bit of harm to anyone, and sure, if it has the effect of easing your worries, then all the better."

Yes, quite a gentle lady, indeed. But it was the last call, almost three weeks ago now, that had decided Sandra against phoning her again. It was a double blow, really, and, bad and all as Mrs. Reynolds' first piece of news was, Sandra was floored by what came after it.

"A heart attack, I'm afraid," said Mrs. Reynolds, as she spoke of her husband's misfortune. "But thank God Cillian still has five months of his year's break from college to go yet. You know, he's every bit as good as his Dad in the shop. Indeed, in the laboratory too. Of course, why wouldn't he be, after three years of science in university. Sure, when I come to think of it, hasn't he been helping his dad in the shop since he was twelve years old. There's hardly anything he doesn't know about the business at this stage."

Sandra still cannot remember whether or not she thought to sympathise with the poor woman. At that point her mind was preoccupied with thoughts of what all of this might mean where Alan was concerned. And, since the phone call, all that she is able to think of is what Cillian may be up to in the laboratory at the back of the Reynolds' shop. Cillian and Alan. Is Alan in on things with Cillian? Certainly, if the conversation in the pub on the day of the court case is anything to go by, she has more than a little reason to think that Alan is up to something.

* * *

The morning traffic tailback is of no great concern to Sandra as she sits behind a van. Low down, near the bumper of the van, there is a white, sphere-shaped disk with a vulgar 'I' blazoned on it. Italy, she thinks, or is that 'IT'? Or maybe Israel? Who knows? What's the abbreviation for Iceland then, she wonders? And India, and God only knows how many others. None of this is of any consequence to her. She is quite happy to sit there in the comfort of her little car and patiently endure the hold-up in the traffic. She thinks of how often over the previous twenty years she has had to listen to Brendan rant on about how they couldn't possibly afford a second car.

"You must be kidding! On a teacher's salary, Sandra! Have you any idea how much it would take to keep a second car? Christ, you must think …"

She smiles to herself now as she visualises him stupidly ranting on. What a difference between him and Matt. None of that dour negativity that seemed to be endemic in Brendan's make-up. In fact, if anything, the opposite is true of Matt: "For God's sake, Sandra, a car! It doesn't have to be a Porsche, you know – just something simple. Sure, you're lost without a car. Relying on buses that, half the time, don't even come; then, when they do, they're bloody-well full. God knows, a car isn't very much to expect. It's the least you might have after all your years of work and doing without."

Even Matt's notion of what constituted work was refreshing, different – indeed, very different to what Brendan thought. Pretty much everything Matt thought was different to Brendan. She still finds it hard to believe, at times, that she said 'Yes' when first he asked her out. Four months ago now. She hardly even knew him at the time. All they had in common was that they worked near each other at the counter in the Credit Union. One on either side of Caroline, the assistant manager in the office. How often they have joked that it is a good thing that Caroline is between them. The thought of it brings another smile to Sandra's lips.

Beep – beep. Bee-bee-bee-beep.

Sandra is jolted from her daydream. Instinctively, she looks up at the rear-view mirror and sees the driver of the car behind throw his hands in the air and nod despairingly. Christ, no wonder. The van from Italy or Israel, or wherever the hell it comes from, is about fifty yards ahead of her. She lets off the handbrake and gently moves forward until she has to stop behind the van again. She turns on the radio, right on time to catch the news. She gets the main headline, but then the traffic starts to move on again, taking away her attention. Then another stop, just in time to catch the final headline.

"The police have launched an inquiry into last night's burning of the Reynolds' Pharmacy in Ballyknock. It took three units of the city fire brigade to bring the fire under control and extensive damage to the building is reported. The Reynolds' Pharmacy is one of the city's few authorised suppliers of the heroin substitute Methadone. No injuries are reported and the cause of the fire is not yet known. A police spokesperson has said that, at this stage, malicious intent cannot be ruled out and that ..."

My God, the Reynolds' Pharmacy, thinks Sandra. As if everything that has happened to them lately hasn't been enough. It is Mrs. Reynolds who comes to Sandra's mind first, then Cillian.

"Cillian!" she says aloud. "Cillian and Alan! Oh, my God! Oh, my God!"

14

Caroline and Matt are in the office when Sandra arrives.

"Good morning," she says, then winks at Matt as she goes by his chair.

"Sandra," says Caroline, "I've just put down the phone. Some guy called Paul O'Keefe was looking for you. He left a number for you to call back. Hold on a second," and, as she says that, she pushes her chair out from the desk and wheels – chair and all – across the office floor to another desk. And, as Caroline crosses the office, Sandra winks at Matt for a second time. He smiles.

"There you go," says Caroline, handing her the yellow sticky-pad page. "Somewhere in the city centre by the look of those numbers."

"Yes, so it would seem. Paul O'…"

"O'Keefe," says Caroline.

Sandra is already punching out the numbers on the phone.

"Paul O'Keefe, Paul O'Keefe," she muses aloud. "God, I haven't the foggiest notion who he might be. Did he give you any idea what it might be ab–"

"Good morning, Pearse Street," comes the voice at the other end of the line, stopping Sandra abruptly in her tracks.

"Pearse Street! The railway station?"

"No, I'm afraid not. This is Pearse Street Garda station."

"Police!" reacts Sandra.

"Was it the railway station you wanted?"

"Well, no. At least, I don't think so. To tell you the truth, I don't really know where I'm meant to be ringing. There was a message left here for me at work to ring your number and to ask for a Paul O'Keefe."

"Ah, Paul. Yes, you've got the right number, all right. Hold the line a moment, please, and I'll put you through. May I ask who's speaking?"

"Yes, my name is Sandra Rogers," then quickly, she adds "or Flynn, maybe."

The man at the end of the line chuckles a little. Sandra knows how strange her answer must sound to him. It is only very recently that she has reverted to using her maiden name. No wonder it sounds confusing to him, she thinks. Sure, she herself is hardly even used to it yet, despite the deliberateness of her decision to use it.

"Flynn, I suppose," she says. Again, there is the hint of a chuckle at the other end, but Sandra knows that there is no malice in it.

"Fine. Hold the line a moment please, Ms. Flynn, and I'll try his office."

He has hardly finished speaking when Sandra finds herself through to Paul O'Keefe.

"Good morning, Mrs. Flynn, this is Paul O'Keefe. I'm a detective here in Pearse Street. Thank you very much for getting back to me so promptly."

Detective, thinks Sandra. There is a momentary silence, an awkwardness more than anything else. Sandra does not know what she should say or if she should say anything at all. But O'Keefe is sensitive towards her being ill at ease.

"Now, Mrs. Flynn, there is absolutely no cause for alarm; let me assure you of that from the outset. It's just that we are holding your son here at the station and I think it would be advisable for you to come down to us."

"Alan!" says Sandra, and immediately the news item she had heard on the car radio comes back to her. Not, indeed, that she had fully managed to dispel it from her mind anyway.

"Yes, Alan. He was brought in here earlier this morning – at 5.58, to be precise – and subsequently had to be taken for stitching in the Outpatients' Department of the Mater Hospital."

"Stitching!" says Sandra, her voice betraying the very anxiety which Paul O'Keefe has been at pains to avoid.

"Yes, but as I said, Mrs. Flynn, there really is no great cause to be worried."

Sandra sighs. It is as if O'Keefe's efforts to put her at ease are only serving to heighten her anxiety.

"Well, what is it, what's wrong?"

"Well, he's fine now, fine. It was minor enough, really, but I do have to tell you that there was a knife involved."

"A knife!" says Sandra, and now her mind is racing even more than ever. "Holy mother of God, are you telling me he has been stabbed?" And then she sighs again, this time far more audibly. And now a silence.

"What I'm trying to impress on you, Mrs. Flynn, is that he really isn't that bad at all. To tell you the truth, it's more of a slash than a stab wound. But I do think that it would be advisable to come over to the station as soon as you can."

There is nothing more said or, to be more precise, Sandra has no memory of anything more being said.

Already, Sandra finds herself amidst the city-centre throng, en route to Pearse Street station. The bars of the dark green railings along the Trinity College wall flit obscurely through her subconscious as they catch the corner of her eye. Her face is ashen and drawn, the prospect of what she may be about to encounter weighing heavily on her mind. Is Alan all right? Are things worse than what Paul O'Keefe has given her to understand? What else is there that he may not have told her? How on earth had the police managed to get a hold of her? All the questions hauntingly visiting themselves on her as she weaves and dodges her way along the footpath. She knew it – she just knew it. As soon as she had heard the news bulletin, something told her that Alan was in the thick of it. Even now, before she has reached the station, she has decided that this knifing and the burning of the Reynolds' Pharmacy are intrinsically tied up with each other.

Beeeeep – be-be-be-beep.

It is the desperate screeching of the bus' brakes as much as the repetitive beeping of the horn that jolts Sandra from the mazy morass into which her mind has descended. Instinctively, she jumps back onto the footpath, her heart thumping against her rib cage now. Christ, only for the sharpness of the bus driver the knifing would be playing second fiddle to an even more serious disaster.

"Jesus, Missus, is the footpath not wide enough for you or what?" the driver bellows out at her. Then he points a finger at the pedestrian light, indicating to her that the little man is still red. His reaction is spontaneous – no real malice or rancour intended. Truth is, he has probably got a far worse shock than Sandra. Now, he just shakes his head in resignation and gingerly moves on.

Sandra is still fairly rattled in herself. She leans against the pole of the pedestrian light and allows herself to absorb exactly what has happened. All of this on top of what is already a serious situation and yet, in a strange way, the jolt has served to dispel the mental stupor which the earlier news of Alan had brought on. There, across the street from her stands the daunting grey-blocked facade of Pearse Street Garda Station. She sighs now, gathers herself, checks that the little green man of the pedestrian light and herself are of one mind, then crosses to the other side.

The policeman she encounters at reception brings her down a long dark corridor. The walls on either side are punctuated with doors. Door after door after door – all closed – and Sandra all the time expecting that the next one will be the one into which they will turn. Of course, when eventually they reach the pertinent door, it is almost at the very end of the corridor.

"Ms. Flynn," announces the policeman from reception, as he opens the door, then stands aside to allow Sandra enter. The first thing she sees is her son. He is sitting dejectedly by a desk, the sizeable gash on his left cheek held together tightly by a row of stitches. The wound looks raw, purpley-red where the stitches are pressing the lips of flesh against each other. Again she sighs. God only knows what her reaction would be were she to learn that this wasn't the first time he had been knifed. Her worries would be more than doubled if she knew of the incident when Ringo Brady gashed his other cheek that night some months back in Mad Benny's. But Alan is cute enough, despite his trouble: he keeps his face turned to one side, only allowing Sandra to see the latest cut. She is no sooner in the office than Paul O'Keefe approaches.

"Mrs. Flynn," he says, extending his right hand to greet her. "I'm Paul O'Keefe. Thank you for coming so quickly." Then he looks at Alan and back to Sandra again. "A moment, please," and, this time, as he speaks, he places his hand on her elbow and intimates that he would like her to step back outside the office.

Outside now, Paul O'Keefe and Sandra walk along the narrow corridor until they reach a row of chairs up at the top end. He gestures to her to sit, then sits down beside her.

"I can't pretend, Mrs. Flynn, that Alan wasn't extremely lucky this time round."

Sandra's confused look in reaction to what he has said is quite obvious to O'Keefe. "You do realise that this is the fourth time in the past three months that Alan has been brought into us here?" Again, it is obvious to him, from the startled look on Sandra's face, that this is the first time she has heard of Alan having had any brush with the law, other than, of course, the occasion which had resulted in the court case.

"I take it, then, that you don't know anything about the previous occasions?"

"No. No, nothing. In fact, I know very little about what's going on in Alan's life at all these days," she says, blurting out what she feels to be half-confession, half-frustration. "I haven't seen him for over nine months – not since the day of the court case last year."

"Hmm! Well, then, obviously we've been seeing quite a lot more of your son than you have. I assume, then, that you know little or nothing of the almost open warfare that is going on among the drug barons in the city centre?"

"Open warfare?" says Sandra, knowing right well that Alan has not exactly been an innocent where the drug question is concerned, but never suspecting until this moment that it might be anything as serious as what Paul O'Keefe seems to be suggesting. She is fairly sure of the nature of the connection between Alan and Cillian, but terms like 'open warfare' and 'drug barons' send shivers down her spine. Taking drugs is one thing, but now it would seem that fears even worse than she had ever contemplated were to be confirmed.

"Yes, Mrs. Flynn, I'm sorry to have to tell you, but Alan is right bang in the middle of it."

"Alan." The utterance suggests more resignation and defeat than it does amazement. Yes, indeed, things are presenting themselves to her in a way that she would least ever want them to do.

"Yes, that's the way things are, I'm afraid," says O'Keefe, knowing that the tone of consolation in his voice can do little to ease the burden which Sandra is feeling.

Sandra has a tightening in her throat and then her tears well up. She leans forward in the chair, raises her hands to her face and begins to cry. O'Keefe is sensitive to the blow that she has taken. There is little he can do for her other than sit there, unwillingly presiding over this purging of sorrow and disappointment. She sobs violently for some minutes and then, as that seems to abate, he discreetly slips a paper handkerchief into her hand, taking care not to make her have to raise her eyes. She sobs a little more from time to time and then, after a while, she musters her courage and turns towards O'Keefe.

"So, what can be done about it?" she asks. "How can he be stopped from doing whatever it is that he is doing?"

"Well, Mrs. Flynn, from your perspective, it isn't that simple to do anything about it. Bear in mind that your son is not a minor. Legally, and in all other respects, he is an independent entity, solely responsible for himself and for anything he does. From what I can gather, he doesn't live with yourself and your husband any longer, so you don't even have any say over him on a domestic level."

Sandra is tempted to tell O'Keefe that Alan is not alone in his absence from home – that Brendan too has been doing his own thing – but, almost as quickly as the notion enters her mind, she dismisses it as being irrelevant to the question in hand. "You must appreciate, Mrs. Flynn, that there is little or nothing the likes of you or I can do in a matter of this sort. Ultimately, it is up to Alan himself to face up to the situation in an honest, manly fashion. That's always how it is where surmounting addiction is concerned. It's pretty much the same as alcoholism: until the person himself acknowledges the problem, there is nothing that anyone else can do about it."

Sandra nods in agreement. O'Keefe's words are an almost perfect reiteration of what the counsellor had had to say when Sandra and Brendan and Alan had first gone to see her. Unfortunately, her words were derisively dismissed by Alan and that derision was handsomely added to by a mixture of indifference and self-protection on the part of Brendan.

"The long and the short of it is that we really don't have any charge that we can level against him here," continues O'Keefe, "and, indeed, even if we did, the reality is that most addicts nowadays are so well up on the finer points of the law that it has become virtually impossible to get them on a charge that is going to stick."

"Well, I'm just at a loss to know what can be done," says Sandra. "I had felt that when he had gone through detox in the unit out in Beaumont that there was, at least, some chance that he might kick th–"

"Detox?" says O'Keefe.

"Yes. Didn't you know that the time he was before the court on charges of possession, he pretty much got off on the basis of his being accepted into the detox unit out at Beaumont?"

"Well, yes, Mrs. Flynn, I am aware of that. But you do, of course, realise that he never actually completed the programme out there."

Sandra feels the blood drain from her face as she listens to O'Keefe, and again, the young detective can see her disappointment. But then, how could Sandra possibly have known? She hasn't even had the advantage of seeing Alan once since the time of the court appearance.

"I'm sorry to be the bearer of such bad tidings, but I just assumed that this was something you would have known," O'Keefe adds, almost as if he is apologising for knowing more about the goings on in her son's life than Sandra. "As I understand it, he was unsettled in the unit from day one, not indeed, that that is all that unusual for an addict. You can imagine yourself how it is for them: constantly seeing other users coming and going, and knowing that it is only a very small minority who leave fully clean."

Sandra nods. All of this has hit her like a bombshell. In her mind, she is feverishly trying to come to terms with this latest snippet of information. Though she had long since put two and two together where Alan and Cillian were concerned, and fully suspected that Alan was into dealing, she had, naively, she supposed now, hoped that, at least, he might not be doing the stuff himself.

"Yes, I'm afraid so, though he did wean himself down a long way before he broke. If memory serves me right," O'Keefe says musingly, "I think he had come down as low as 15 ml before he did a runner. Sometimes, you know, they can get so close to being completely clean that the prospect of facing life without a fix scares the living daylights out of them. That may sound strange to you, but all the research shows that, very often, that's just the way it is."

Again, Sandra can do nothing more than nod.

"I'm sorry, Mrs. Flynn, I thought you would have already known all of this. I wouldn't have it in such detail myself except that I rang Beaumont this morning to see if they might have a contact number for you. I presume it was Alan who gave them your number at the time. That, in itself, would have been a very positive sign."

Another nod from Sandra.

"Was that your daughter then who answered your phone at home? She gave me your work number."

"Yes, Naomi," says Sandra, barely managing to get the words out before bursting into tears for a second time.

Again Paul O'Keefe places a hand on Sandra's elbow – some small gesture of support. They both stand then and begin to walk back down the corridor. O'Keefe suggests that perhaps a little fresh air would not be a bad idea. Huh, the thought of it – a hefty inhalation of good old carbon dioxide that passes as city air. Still, the change itself might not do any harm. Outside now, the world of personal pursuits mixes with the din of city traffic to drown the telltale signs of embarrassment.

"Anyway, it isn't as if you could have been sure that he would have stayed clean even if he had seen the detox programme to completion," says O'Keefe.

Sandra looks at him. Again, the thought that this young man knows so much more about her son than she herself knows only serves to enhance her sense of despair.

"Not that it can be any source of consolation to you, but, you know, fully ninety-seven per cent of addicts go back on the stuff within a year of detox," he tells her.

"Ninety-seven per cent," repeats Sandra.

"Yeah, that's what all the evidence suggests, Mrs. Flynn. So, you see how really difficult it is to kick the habit once it has taken a hold of you."

Then, there is fully a half-minute's silence before either speaks again. "I don't know whether or not you heard the morning news?" O'Keefe says, "But it was really something other than the actual knifing itself that prompted me to ask you to call by to see me."

Immediately, the mounting tension is all too obvious again in Sandra's face. She knew, she just knew that Alan was somehow tied up with the burning of the pharmacy!

"Reynolds' Pharmacy, you mean?" she says.

"Yes, so you have heard it. Perhaps we'd be better to go back inside to discuss it in Alan's presence," he suggests.

"Yes, I think so, Pa ..." and she stops herself just in time from using his first name.

"Paul is fine," he says, and he smiles kindly at her.

"Yes, well, I think so, Paul. There really isn't much sense in us discussing it without him."

"Just one last thing before we do go back inside, Mrs. Flynn. I sense from our discussion that you really aren't that fully aware of the urgency of what is going on at the moment."

The look on Sandra's face is sufficient to assure him that his suspicion is correct.

"Things in this city are at boiling point – far beyond a point that they have ever reached before," he begins. "There is a vicious struggle going on between the inner city drug barons and, given the current level of tension, something like a knifing, or even a killing, won't cost them a second thought if it means protecting the tidy rackets they have going."

Sandra is aghast as she listens to him, her eyes wide and fear-filled. Paul O'Keefe then extends his hand towards the entrance again and they go back down the long narrow passageway.

This time, as they walk, Sandra has much more of a sense of where she is going. Paul O'Keefe's office door is wide open when they reach it and, as they enter, they find that Alan is no longer there. Sandra and O'Keefe look despairingly at each other and, though nothing is said, they both realise that Alan's absence does not bode well.

15

A crowded Mad Benny's later that night. The din is deafening and the place, as ever, is packed with dancers. There is nothing to distinguish this particular night from any other except, perhaps, that the name of the day is different to that which went before it. The three Bradys are upstairs on the balcony – Ringo holding court, while his brothers, Tommo and Dessie, listen to him attentively. No sign of Johnny or Cillian on the balcony, or even Alan for that matter. That particular trio is downstairs in Johnny's office, combing over the disaster of Cillian's father's place having been burnt down the night before. Johnny is slouched back in his wheely-chair with his feet resting on top of the desk, while Cillian is nervously pacing up and down the little office. Alan has his backside half-perched on the edge of Johnny's desk and, with the exception of the odd contribution to the conversation, is very much the minnow in what's being discussed.

"Jesus, there was hundreds of thousands worth of stuff made up. Fucking E and Smack and God only knows what else. Top-grade gear fucking burnt to nothing, the fuckers. Eight hundred thousand euro worth, at least, maybe nine. What do you think, Alan?"

"Easily nine hundred thousand, maybe a million," says Alan.

"Christ, weeks of work down the fucking drain. So, what the fuck do we do now then, Johnny? Can you tell me that, can you?"

"Easy on, Cillian, boy. You're getting way too uptight about all this."

Cillian stops his pacing and stares hard at Johnny. He can't believe he's hearing this.

"Too fucking uptight? Of course, I'm fucking-well uptight. How the fuck would you be about it if it was your old man's place and they put a fucking torch to it? How about that then, Johnny, huh?"

Johnny shifts his feet off the desk with bewildering speed and, at the same time, pulls open the desk drawer, whips out a flick-knife and pushes Cillian back against the office door. A torrent of movement, very much at variance with Johnny's laid-back demeanour up to then.

"What the fuck is that supposed to mean then, Cillian, boy, what? Is that meant to be some sort of a fucking threat then, is it? Is it, Cillian?" and, as he fires the questions, he has his forearm pressed hard against Cillian's windpipe and the blade of the flick-knife held threateningly near his face.

Alan is totally taken aback by this explosion of activity from Johnny and is only getting to his feet now, having been brushed off the desk and knocked to the ground as Johnny had surged forward. The white light of the overhead neon tube is catching the blade of the knife and is dancing threateningly in it as Johnny twirls it under Cillian's nose. The movement has been frenzied and frenetic, and all that Alan can think is that it is as close to something out of 'Psycho' as he could possibly imagine.

"Jesus, Johnny, take it easy, man," says Alan, somewhat apprehensively, the sense of nervousness and uncertainty all too obvious in his voice. Johnny, keeping Cillian pinned back with his forearm, turns his head towards Alan. His eyes are filled with madness.

"And you shut your fucking kisser, you stupid little bollocks."

Alan can almost feel himself jumping back in shock, fearful, more than anything else, that Johnny's whole attention might as easily be diverted onto him. But then Johnny turns back towards Cillian and presses that little bit harder against his windpipe.

"Now, Cillian, baby, would you like to be a little bit more specific in what you're saying?" he says, menacingly twirling the tip of the flick-knife inside the opening of one of Cillian's nostrils. The madness Alan has already seen in Johnny's eyes is even more obvious to Cillian. His own eyes are focused down on the knife's blade as he watches Johnny rotate it in little circles within the nostril. Cillian can feel the coldness of sweat on his forehead and now his breathing is causing the inside of his nostril to occasionally make contact with the edge of the blade.

"Jesus, Johnny, take it easy," he says. "I didn't mean it as a threat, man. You know I didn't, honest to God, man." The words trip hesitantly from Cillian's lips, as he desperately tries to assure Johnny that he has taken him up wrongly. Then Cillian senses some easing of the pressure on his neck – or, at least, he thinks he does, he hopes he does. Alan too senses that Johnny has backed off a little.

"As long as we're fucking clear on that, man. No fucking threats, you get me? I don't like being fucking-well threatened, Cillian, baby. Dig?"

"Yeah, Johnny, yeah. No threats, no problem."

Then Johnny shifts his gaze back to Alan, who jumps almost as badly as he had done before. "Jesus, yeah, Johnny, no problem, no problem at all, just as Cillian says."

Johnny grimaces, then the grimace turns to a sneer and he eases all pressure on Cillian's neck and backs away from him. The clicking sound of the blade re-embedding itself inside the black casing suggests that the danger has passed and, as Johnny throws the knife back into the drawer and closes it, it is almost possible to hear the sighs of relief from the other two.

"So, then, Alan, baby, what happened to your pretty little face?" says Johnny, as he runs his fingernail along the cut on Alan's cheek. The suddenness of the touch makes Alan wince and immediately pull back. He knows that Johnny has deliberately dug a little with his fingernail, but he daren't react too strongly towards him. The last thing he needs is to occasion a repeat performance of Johnny's earlier outburst. Alan holds his hand to the wound and can already feel it pumping.

"Aw, it's nothing, just a little bit of a fracas I got into last night."

"A little bit of a fracas! Jaysus, you better not have too many of them or it's going to become very hard to look at you," says Johnny, and he emits that ugly croak of a laugh which is so much a defining feature of his. Alan always thinks it is the nearest thing to an ass braying he has ever heard. In fact, right now he feels very much like saying so to Johnny but, as usual, he doesn't have the balls to stand up to him. The fucking cheek of Johnny, anyway, thinks Alan, particularly in view of all the lines he has on his own ugly mug. But he bites his tongue and has to make do with cursing Johnny within the safety of his mind.

A timely ringing of the phone draws Johnny's attention away from the immediacy of the situation and serves, for the time being, to diffuse the tension.

"Hello," barks Johnny.

The other two look over at each other, each realising that it is wisest to keep things on an even keel for now. As they look back at Johnny on the phone, they can hear the unintelligible cackle at the other end of the line.

"Who said so?" bellows Johnny, and as he asks the question, he looks at Cillian and Alan.

"Who fucking said that?" he barks again, leaning forward abruptly in his seat and suddenly reddening in the face.

"Frank!" he says, obviously having received an answer to his question.

Again, Cillian and Alan look across at each other, aware that there is a sudden heightening of tension in the air. Next thing Johnny jumps up out of his seat and now his face is even redder than it had been.

"Well, you tell that little bollocks to go screw himself. I'm the fucking gaffer in this joint and I call the fucking shots on what goes down here. Twig?"

More cackling at the far end of the line, then Johnny snaps.

"Put a fucking sock in it, pal. Zip it or I'll have it fucking-well zipped up for you. Now get your bloody arse up here in a hurry." And, with that, Johnny smashes the receiver down into its cradle.

"Holy Christ!" he roars, and the whiteness of the bone is visible in his fingers where he has pressed them down hard against the desktop. Then he turns and furiously kicks the wastepaper basket to the far end of the office. "Fucking chancers," he says. He sighs, a long slow sigh, and looks at his two comrades. They aren't too sure what is the best thing to do, whether to say something or simply hold their peace.

"Is there –?"

"You shut it, Cillian. Just fucking shut it," says Johnny. "I'm fucking sick and tired of your fucking whinging and whining. Now, just put a fucking stopper in it for once, will you, and let me think a second."

And then, before Johnny even has a chance to

contemplate whatever it is that has so enraged him, there is a knock on the office door.

"In!" he barks.

A second knock.

"In, fucking in, I said, you stupid bollocks. Are you fucking deaf or what?" and he lunges at the door, opens it and pulls the teenager into the room.

"Now, you, what's all this shite you're going on with about there being no water in the gaff?"

The young lad is obviously scared stiff and doesn't know quite what it is he has done to so enrage his boss. He stands nervously in the middle of the office, the reflection of the overhead light seeming to enhance the fear filling his eyes.

"No-no, Johnny," he begins nervously. "It's n-not that there's no water. It's that it has been turned off."

"Jaysus, no fucking water or water turned off – what the fuck's the difference? Get your arse back down there and do something about it. For Christ sake, it isn't even eleven o'clock yet and if that fucking water is off before we have those bottles out on the stands, there won't be a single dancer within an ass's roar of this place. They'll all be down the road in The Starlight. Now go!"

"But Frank said –"

"And tell Frank to get himself up here double quick and he better be toting a fucking-good explanation for all of this with him."

"But, Johnny –"

"But, Johnny nothing. Tell him, I said."

"But, Johnny, Frank didn't have anything to do with it." The young lad quickly spills out this jewel of information before Johnny can interrupt him again. And now there is a weighty silence in the office, each one of the four looking from one to the other. Then Johnny turns back towards the teenager and, in a pedantic measured tone, asks, "What the fuck are you playing at, boy? I thought you shagging-well told me on the phone that it was Frank who turned it off."

"Well, yeah, I did, Johnny, but that was only because the Bradys made him do it."

"The Bradys!" says Johnny. " But sure, the Bradys and myself have an arrang–"

"Yeah, Johnny, Ringo Brady came down and told him to knock it off and to put out the bottle stands."

Silence fills the room again but, this time, it is more the product of incredulity than anger. Johnny's eyes latch on to Cillian's and from there to Alan's, then finally to the poor unfortunate who has been summoned to the office. His own patch – Johnny the Fix's own little patch – being stepped on by the Bradys, and Johnny doesn't like it.

"Out!" barks Johnny, "out!" The teenager is hesitant, afraid to move, yet knowing he isn't meant to stay.

"Out," I said, "out, out, out, get fucking out!" and Johnny grabs him and roughly bundles him out. He slams the door shut and turns, pressing his back hard against it, to look at Cillian and Alan.

"Shite on it," he says. "Shite and more shite."

16

At this stage, Sandra's feet are working on autopilot as she tos and fros up and down the kitchen floor. If she has crossed the floor once, she must have done so a thousand times. What, in the name of God, is Brendan at that he hasn't rung yet? Her first effort to get him was earlier this morning and that was from Detective O'Keefe's office. And, of course, wouldn't you know it! Today of all days, he is on a training course. God, and all the times over the years she has heard him complain of how little opportunity there is for training of teachers of German. But still, the secretary at the school – Amy's stand-in – had said it was just a morning course, that he would be back to work in the afternoon. She assured Sandra she would pass on the message that she had rung. Sandra had left both home and work numbers with her.

Then, when no call had come by six o'clock, she rang his apartment. He wasn't there either. It was Amy who answered. This was the first time Sandra had spoken to her since Brendan and she had moved in together. She knew Amy was very near her time, but deliberately didn't ask her how the pregnancy was going. She simply gave her the details of the situation and asked that Brendan phone her as soon as he came in.

Sandra glances at the kitchen clock now: 11.13pm. She sighs. What could possibly be delaying him until this hour? Matt reaches out and takes hold of her hand as she passes. He squeezes it gently. He has stayed with her since finishing work this afternoon. If nothing else, he can provide some moral support for her. He hasn't even met Alan. All he really knows of him is what Sandra has told him over the previous few months. He doesn't know Brendan from Adam either. The prospect that things being as they are may necessitate their finally meeting each other tonight has him a little nervous. But that is something he will handle if it serves in any way to ease Sandra's burden.

And Sandra – she is more than aware of how very lucky she is to have Matt. She can think of many a man who would have done a runner as soon as there was the slightest sign of trouble. Particularly drugs. But not Matt. She bends down now and kisses him on the forehead, then continues her pacing. Another look over at the clock. Good God almighty, not even eleven fifteen yet. How time drags when there's something hanging over you, she thinks.

"Why don't you sit down a while, love," suggests Matt, "take a rest." It is the first time either of them has spoken in the past five or six minutes. Sandra sighs again, comes to one of the kitchen chairs and eases herself down onto it. She is hardly seated when the phone rings. Immediately, she stands and makes for the phone, lifting the receiver before it even rings a second time.

"Yes," she says. That in itself is somewhat ironic, given that she was forever chastising Alan for answering the phone in just that fashion.

"Sandra!"

"Brendan! Oh, Brendan, thank God you've rung at last." She puts her hand across the mouthpiece and mimes to Matt that it is Brendan, almost as though Matt would not have realised that when he heard her say the name.

"What kept you so long in ringing back, Brendan? I've been waiting to hear from you since morning."

Matt thinks to himself how irrelevant it is at this stage what has kept Brendan so long in ringing. The main thing is that he has finally made contact. Sandra is now into the throes of telling her estranged husband of the morning's events and how worried for Alan's welfare she is in view of all that Paul O'Keefe has told her of the warring going on between the drug barons.

"And if what he says is right, Alan is caught up in the middle of it," she says.

They talk for quite some time, discussing what is best for them to do, eventually coming to the conclusion that, when all is said and done, there is abysmally little that they can do to alter the situation. Nothing for it but to sit tight and wait, and let matters take their course.

"No, I'm not. Naomi is asleep, but Matt is here with me," says Sandra, obviously in answer to Brendan having asked if she is alone. Matt wasn't sure until now whether or not Brendan was even aware of his existence.

Then there is the small talk that so often heralds the end of a conversation and they both hang up, affirming once again that the best they can do is to sit it out and wait. The frustration of this being the only course open to her is visibly weighing on Sandra as she comes back towards the table.

"I'm afraid you're right though, Sandra, love," says Matt. "All you really can do is wait. Wait and pray, that's all."

She nods and then forlornly eases herself onto the chair again. And now the tears well up in her eyes.

"How about a cup of coffee?" asks Matt, trying to generate some enthusiasm in his speech in the vain hope that this may somehow better the situation. Sandra nods her head in response, then raises her hand to stop the falling tears.

* * *

"What the fuck do you think you're up to here, Frank – what?"

"Johnny!"

"Fuck the Johnny crap, Frank. Just what the hell do you think you're at?"

Frank is visibly rattled in Johnny's presence, his eyes flitting nervously from Cillian to Alan, who stand either side of the night-club owner. The only possible protection that Frank senses is the table between himself and the other three, on which there stands a bevy of plastic water bottles. Johnny looks at the bottles and immediately recognises them as someone's other than his own. He raises one and shoves it up very close to Frank's face.

"So, what the fuck is this then, Frank?"

"A bottle of water, Joh–"

"I know it's a fucking bottle of water, you stupid little bollocks. What I want to know is what the fuck are you doing selling the fucker?" Johnny's face reddens with anger as he speaks, red as a beetroot except for the finely lined scars of the Slish-Slash, which stand out in white relief against the darker flesh.

"The Bradys said to –"

"The Bradys, the Bradys! I've had it up to fucking here about the whoring Bradys. Who the fuck do you think you're working for then, Frank?" Johnny bellows at the youngster. Then he reaches over to him, grabs him by the shirt and pulls him halfway across the table, sending bottles rolling every which way.

"Well, Frank, who?"

"You, Johnny, you."

Their noses are almost touching and Frank's eyes are bulging with fear.

"And who pays your fucking wages, boy, who?"

"You do, Johnny, you do." The tremble in Frank's voice suggests he is on the verge of crying.

"That's right, Frank, I do. And you better fucking remember that in future if you want to keep on working here," and Johnny pushes the boy away from him, then flings the bottle of water that he had picked up earlier with all his might into his midriff. He then grabs his side of the table and turns it upside down, sending plastic bottles in all directions – some down on top of Frank and others hopping out across the floor.

"Get rid of those fucking bottles before I fucking kill someone," he bellows at Cillian and Alan, then turns and looks up at the balcony. The Brady brothers are standing at the railing, watching. They've seen everything. There is a slight reddening in Ringo Brady's face above. A frenzied look in Johnny's face below.

"Come on, you two, forget about the bloody bottles," says Johnny, and he makes for the spiral staircase with Cillian and Alan in tow behind him.

The Bradys are standing threateningly, waiting on the balcony when the others reach the top of the stairs. Somehow, Johnny's courage isn't quite what it had been when he was down at ground-floor level, but he knows he cannot afford to let the Bradys see any uncertainty in his face. He tightens his mouth, not realising that Ringo Brady has seen the deliberateness of that action and that he already knows Johnny's feet are considerably colder than they had been.

What is ominously worse for all three – Johnny, Cillian and Alan – is that they haven't the slightest idea that the Bradys have knives concealed in their jacket sleeves. The brothers back away a little, an old and well-learned ploy to suck their victims in. They back off even more now, so that their bodies are pressed against the balcony railings. The Bradys are hefty men and they each focus a fixed stare at the Mad Benny trio. Johnny's eyes are flitting tellingly from one brother to the next. Cillian and Alan are even worse again, each of them looking towards Johnny for reassurance when the whole focus of their attention should be on Ringo and his brothers.

Johnny 'The Fix' Hellerman is feeling increasingly under pressure. He hasn't exactly stormed up to the balcony for a cup of tea, but, now that he is there, he knows he doesn't really have the balls to do what needs doing. When eventually he makes his move, it is neither a walk nor a surge but something in between, which betrays his self-belief. It would be so much better for himself if he was just an out-and-out coward, but this way he is mere fodder for the Bradys.

Two of the brothers part a little as Johnny makes for them, each pulling back an arm, and then, just as Johnny reaches them, they bring forward their arms again and drive their knives hard into his stomach. Suddenly, Johnny's body is fixed rigid, suspended on the knives, his eyes bulging and his view out across the balcony railing of the dancers below obscure and hazy and blackening by the second. And now there is no light, no dancers, no thumping of music in Johnny's ears. He falls face down onto the floor.

Cillian is fixed to the spot as he watches all of this, while Alan is beside himself with fear. Somehow, somewhere, Alan finds it in himself to make a dart for the spiral staircase, but Tommo Brady is far too fast for him. Too strong for him too. He grabs Alan, hauls him back across the balcony and throws him onto one of the seats where they had been sitting before the whole fracas about the water erupted. Alan sits there, afraid to move and even more afraid of what may be about to happen to him.

Now Dessie and Ringo Brady make for Cillian. He tries to back away from them, but they up the pace, grab a leg and an arm apiece and sweep him across to the balcony railing. Cillian is screaming frantically – so frantic that the dancers below can hear his shouts above the music. They look up towards the balcony to see what is going on and, as they do, they see the Bradys holding Cillian out across the railing. All they can really see is his back and legs but, immediately, Carole recognises who they are holding.

"Cillian!" she screams, as she looks up. The scream is long and shrill, far louder even than Cillian's own scream some moments earlier. And then the Brady brothers drop him.

As Carole watches, it is as though Cillian's fall to the floor is happening in slow motion. The dancers, too, stand helplessly watching this mass of flesh – arms and legs flailing frantically – come towards them. And then the thud, right in the centre of the dance floor.

Immediately the dancers scatter, most of them heading for one or other exit door, eager to be off the premises before the cops arrive on the scene. There is pandemonium in the hall as they climb over one another to get out. The rotating multicoloured lights only serve to add to the sense of panic that has gripped them. And then, in no time, they are gone.

One solitary person approaches the human mound in the centre of the floor. Poor Carole. She goes down on her knees, presses her cheek against the back of Cillian's head and emits a long heart-rending cry. Placing her hands beneath his head, she turns Cillian's face towards her. His body, already cooling, will soon be as cold as marble, his mind oblivious to the music that still pumps away as ever.

And Carole doesn't even know yet that Johnny's body lies inert on the floor of the balcony above.

"Come on, let's get our arses out of here," says Ringo to his brothers, "and take that little bastard along with you," and he nods towards Alan. "Here, Dessie," he adds, throwing the bag of E tabs to his brother, "take them with you and pump a rake of them into the little fucker on the way."

17

The first thing that hits Alan as he opens his eyes is the smell of dampness filling his nostrils. Then, as he starts to adapt to his surroundings, he also begins to make sense of the light bulb overhead. Though uncomfortable, its light is dim, just about enough for him to realise that what is rotating slowly above his head is, in fact, the ceiling. He closes his eyes, then opens them again, hoping, somehow, that this will serve to dispel the discomfort, but the ceiling still appears to rotate. The only difference now is that he has become very aware of a burning sensation all across his face. He tries to raise his right hand to feel his cheek, but finds he cannot do so. Slowly, he turns his head to the right and sees the ropes that are tying him down to whatever it is he is lying on – a camp-bed of some sort. The effort to turn his head fills his face with pain. He waits now for the pain to recede and, as he waits, he ponders whether or not he will look to his left. Then, a turn to the left: more ropes, more pain, again that searing, burning sensation all across his face. My God, it's just so incredibly sore.

"Hey, boys, the hard man Alan is back with us again," he hears from somewhere in the room. His first thought is to try to raise his head to see who has spoken, but the thought of the pain again is sufficient to deter him. Then, the figure of a man stands over him, crossing his line of vision and obscuring the discomfort of the glaring light bulb overhead. The man lowers himself onto his hunkers and draws his face right up close to Alan's. Ringo Brady.

"You're coming down, Alan, baby," Ringo sneers, as he holds an empty syringe up to Alan's face. There is no way that Alan can possibly know that they have pumped so many E tabs into him and followed that with a hefty fix of heroin. And, despite the heroin, his face is filled with pain.

"But, by Christ, have we had some fun with you, boy, as you've been coming down," says Tommo Brady, as he too now steps into Alan's range of vision. Alan can see that Tommo is also holding something in his hand, but he cannot quite make out what it is. The youngest of the brothers then stoops down by the side of Alan's head and Alan corners his eyes to see what it is he is holding. Even the pain of trying to turn his eyes goes through him like a scythe and then, the horrific realisation of what Tommo has in his hand. Christ, a knife! A very finely tipped knife.

"Slish-Slash," says Tommo, coming up very close to Alan's face and, as he says the words, he makes a fast criss-cross movement with the blade, then bursts into laughter. His open mouth seems inordinately big to Alan, his teeth all yellow and uneven, and there are ugly black hairs sticking out from the darkness of his nostrils.

Alan closes his eyes, hoping, somehow, to escape the nightmare. Despite the fix of Smack, his face feels so unbelievably sore, especially on the right side. He feels like crying, but will not allow himself to do so. Maybe he's dreaming; maybe it's all a nightmare, a subconscious cocktail of all the ugly stuff that has been going on in his life. Maybe, any second now, he's going to wake up and find that the worst of anything that is happening to him is that he is pouring sweat at the thought that any of this could possibly be true. And now, he opens his eyes again and finds that no, he isn't dreaming.

Then Dessie Brady comes into view. "And that's not anything compared to what's to come, Flynnie-boy," says Dessie, and then he laughs. "We're really going to give you a high time," he says, opening a fistful of dirty brown, powdery Skag so that Alan can see the tablets. Then all three Bradys go into convulsions of laughter, throwing back their heads and, once again, everything takes on a distorted look for Alan.

Now Ringo draws his face up close to Alan's once again, puts his thumb against Alan's cheek, then grinds it hard into his flesh, breaking the hard, crusted lines of blood and opening the wounds again. The pain is excruciating, far worse than anything Alan has ever felt before, far worse than anything he could even have imagined feeling. He screams with pain, the writhing of his body restricted by the ropes that tie him down. And, as he screams, Dessie Brady pushes the rounded Skag tabs into Alan's mouth, almost as if he is feeding a one-armed bandit, then holds Alan's mouth tightly shut. Alan does not have the strength to fight Dessie's hold on him and certainly is in no position to spew the tablets back out again. He knows that whatever is to happen now is entirely in someone else's hands.

* * *

2.42am. Sandra's head rests on Matt's shoulder as they sit on the settee. It's a quarter of an hour or so since Sandra eventually fell off to sleep. Matt is reluctant to waken her to take her upstairs to bed. She is better left as she is for now, he figures, to get whatever benefit there is from her sleep. However uncomfortable it may be, it has to be better than no sleep at all. Despite Matt's care in easing his arm out from under her to look at his watch, he disturbs her.

"Mmm!" she says, stirring a little, then half-opening her eyes. She looks dozy. Matt places his thumb against the corner of her mouth and rubs away the saliva that has trickled out as she slept. She can feel pins and needles in her arm from being nestled in under Matt's shoulder for so long. And now her eyes are fully open.

"Oh, Matt, what time is it at all?"

"Nearly a quarter to three, love."

Matt can see her lighting up a little. He knows what is on the tip of her tongue. "No, no news yet, love," he says, even before she asks the question.

Her face falls. She nestles into Matt again. At this stage, she no longer has the energy to cry.

"Come on, love, you'd be far better off in bed where you'd get a proper sleep instead of all this nodding off and wakening up again."

She nods submissively.

"I can stay down here for now and, if any news comes through, I'll waken you immediately. What do you say?"

"Okay, Matt," and she nuzzles him.

Then Matt stands and helps her up off the settee and out towards the stairs.

"That's far better than sitting there, not knowing where he is and, what's worse again, not being able to do anything about it anyway. Isn't it?"

* * *

"Is it heated yet?" asks Ringo Brady.

"Nearly there. Only another couple of seconds," replies Tommo, as he holds the spoon steady over the flame and watches the light dance in the liquid that fills its belly.

The walls of the room are dank and dingy and, as far as the dimness of the light allows, they seem to be smeared with a mixture of graffiti and of stale and splattered blood. Dessie Brady is busy, meticulously finishing off the job on

Alan's other cheek.

"Here, here's the tourniquet. Get a move on, will you," says Ringo, nudging Dessie as he works away on Alan's face.

"Well, fuck you, Ringo," he says, regaining his balance and hurrying to clean away the smearing that his brother's nudge has caused.

"Christ, you'd think it was the fucking Mona Lisa you were working on," says Tommo.

"Fuck up, the two of you!" barks Ringo. Immediately there is silence. "The tourniquet," he says to Dessie again, "put it on his left arm this time and get a fucking good vein up." Dessie begins to do as he's been told.

"Syringe," demands Ringo, holding up his right hand like a surgeon in an operating theatre. Then Tommo reaches over to him and hands him the syringe.

"How's the Smack coming along?"

"Nearly there, Ringo. Just letting her back off the heat again."

"Come on then, give it over to me," says Ringo, impatiently.

Tommo hunches down beside his brother now and Ringo eases the tip of the needle into the darkened liquid until the eye is deep down into it, then gently, steadily, he draws the plunger slowly towards him and watches the barrel of the syringe fill.

There is a golden gleam now to the liquid inside the barrel. Ringo raises the syringe up against the light, then lowers it back down again and leans in over Alan. Alan is almost totally spaced – sweaty, feverish, fidgety, now that the Skag is doing a number on him, yet all this time restricted by the ropes that hold him firmly down on the camp-bed. His eyes, though bulging in their sockets, have a gauzy veneer across them, totally concealing the panic he must feel within.

"Now, Flynnie, sonny," says Ringo into Alan's ear, "no more fucking around with Ringo Brady, boy." Then Ringo breaks the skin of Alan's left arm with the needle tip and eases the dragon's blood into the vein.

Ringo watches as the liquid in the barrel empties itself into the young man, then yanks the needle out and, as he flings it across the room, he sits back against the wall and bursts out laughing. His brothers join him in his laughter now, but Alan is oblivious to it all.

"Toss me over one of those cans, Tommo," says Ringo, as the laughter subsides. Then, when his brother throws a can of lager to him, Ringo catches it, momentarily holds it up towards the light, pulls the ring to open and sprays all around him as it explodes out of the can. Most of it seems to land on Alan's face, mixing with the crusted blood that has formed on it and causing it to run in pinkish streamlets down his neck. Then Ringo takes a swig from the can, eases it away from his mouth again and smacks his lips.

"Jesus, and to think there are some poor fuckers who go for junk instead of this," he says, and he holds the can back up towards the light again. And all three go into kinks of laughter.

* * *

It is shortly before six in the morning when Sandra is woken by the screeching of a car. She is just coming to terms with what it is she has heard when it is followed by the sound of a thud against the front door. Good God almighty! She hops out of bed, quickly looks into Naomi's bedroom, then scurries down the stairs. The sitting-room door is wide open and inside, on the settee, Matt is fast asleep, obviously unaware of any noise. Sandra is tempted to waken him, but then thinks better of it. It may all be for nothing and, anyway, he is there at hand if she should need him.

She walks towards the front door and opens it slowly. Oh my God! There before her on the doorstep is a sizeable sack – one of the old hemp type – filled with something and barely closed at the top. She can feel her heart racing within her rib cage and all she can think of is that terrifying night at the start of all this trouble when she had found Alan lying against the door. Oh, God, no, she thinks, but already she knows it is Alan. Immediately now, she thinks again of waking Matt but then, almost as quickly, for some reason that she cannot discern, she decides not to.

She stoops and unties the rope holding the mouth of the sack half-closed. The first thing she sees is a head of hair, wet and dark and tacky, and, as she opens more, Alan's head falls to one side and bangs against the concrete doorstep.

A scream …

18

The day of the funeral. The Mass over, they have come to the graveside, all gathered round to look into the blackness of the hole into which Alan Flynn's body will be lowered, then never seen again.

The young priest officiating is busy talking to the undertaker at the edge of the grave; they are discussing something humorous, or so their grins suggest. Then, as they move away from each other, their grins turn into laughter. The priest gathers himself again, looks more solemn for some seconds, but is distracted then by an itch on the calf of his leg. As he scratches vigorously, he also manages to take stock of those assembled. And now the vestiges of solemnity turn visibly to impatience. He looks behind him abruptly and eyes the stragglers still making their way towards the graveside. A deliberate look at his watch, a little cough and then, "In the name of the Father and of the Son and of the Holy Spirit ..."

Sandra instinctively makes the Sign of the Cross but, thereafter, her mind absents itself from the ritual of the occasion. It isn't that she does not wish to partake, and indeed to fully partake, in the parting of her son. The parting of her son. In a funny way, she had had a premonition that first day ever that she had found the sordid rubber tubing and other implements under Alan's bed that this is how things would end. Thinking on it now, she figures Fate has had an awful lot to do with what has happened. Even if Brendan had been interested enough to involve himself as fully as he should have done, things would not have turned out any differently, she thinks.

She can sense Naomi drawing in ever closer to her by the graveside. Matt is there too, his hand supportively placed across her back. She is vulnerable, brittle, reduced by all she has endured. It is almost a week since she has been told that an autopsy would be necessary. The wait since then until the burial has taken a heavy toll on her. And even today, she knows, is more of a beginning than an end. The beginning of memories, of mental anguish, of pain – a different pain. But Naomi will be there alongside her. And Matt.

At the other side of the grave stands Brendan, with Amy beside him. As Sandra looks over at them, she is struck by how startlingly good-looking Amy is, despite her being so far gone in her pregnancy. Far younger looking than Brendan, thinks Sandra, but then, of course, she is little more than half his age. And Brendan himself – he looks bereft and broken, his eyes fixed firmly on the black hole where his son will go. Sandra knows, no matter what was or wasn't done, that Alan's death is gnawing at him. He is probably suffering more than she is, she thinks. Who knows?

Sandra's thinking is occasionally impinged upon by the priest's words. Despite his comparative youth, he is rattling off the prayers like he's an old hand at it. Indeed, he's probably not even that much older than Alan himself. Hardly ten years between the two of them, she thinks. He's surely no more than thirty. Her Alan never saw thirty, not even twenty. Certainly won't see either of them now.

Didn't, doesn't, won't, she thinks – all of it an unassembled mish-mash in her mind. Years of teasing out and self-questioning ahead of her. A lifetime of it, really. If she had done this or that, would things have been any different? What if she had been more alert to things? Would it have been better to ...? And then, after every bout of anguish and questioning, she will find out that there are no answers – none that will satisfy, at any rate. And that's all that lies ahead.

Now, unexpectedly, she finds the priest standing right in front of her, one hand grasping her hand and the other holding her at the elbow. He must have been several seconds there before his presence has even registered with her.

"May the Good Lord give you the strength and grace to carry the burden he has placed upon you, Sandra" and, once again, the solemnity with which he speaks his priestly words seems far more in keeping with a man who is twice his age. "I will remember yourself and the family in my prayers."

Sandra sobs bitterly as he stands before her. All she can do is nod and draw Naomi even closer to her with her free hand. Matt's hand is still on her back, supporting, trying to console. The priest moves on to Naomi, places his hand on top of her head and says something – a prayer, perhaps – that isn't clearly heard by anyone but himself. Then he takes himself across to the other side to sympathise with Brendan and Amy.

And now the stream of people lining up, one after the other, to convey their condolences to Sandra. She stands inertly and receives them. All she sees are coats – grey, brown, navy, white and God only knows what other colours. It's strange that that is what should register so strongly with her, rather than words or faces. Stranger still, though Sandra has no way of knowing it at this stage, is the fact that it is that, more than many other facets of this day, which will stay in her memory for years to come. That and hands.

Yet another hand grips her's now, but somehow, this

particular hand arouses an alertness in her. It feels far softer than any of the others she has shaken.

"I'm very sorry for your trouble, Mrs. Flynn. I'm Carole, a friend of Alan's."

Sandra looks into the fresh young face before her. She remembers her from the pub on the day of the court case. There is a gentleness about her and youthfulness in her face – the same youthfulness that had been so much a part of Alan. In a way, Sandra feels a smidgen of jealousy towards this beautiful young woman who had so much more contact with Alan than she herself has had in the past year or so. But much greater than any jealousy she feels is some form of affection she senses towards her. It's strange she should feel that, she thinks, given that her only previous contact with her was nothing if not scant. Sandra closes both hands around Carole's hand now and squeezes kindly, and the tears mount in her eyes.

"Carole," she says, "Carole." And, with that, the young woman is gone and someone else has stepped into her place.

Sandra is startled by the roughness of this new hand and yet the feel of Carole's is still very much with her. That softness. It is hard for her to think that, somewhere, there are other hands – hands so cruel that the extent of their sympathy might be to carve up the face of some mother's son and leave him dead.

Ringo Brady stands well back to the rear of the crowd. It is insult enough that he has even dared to show his face at the funeral. Thank God Sandra doesn't know who he is or that he's even there. Thank God too, that, brazen as he is, he is not so brazen that he would come forward to sympathise with her – to place his hand in hers. That, at least, is one memory she will be spared.

ECSTASY
and other stories
by
Ré Ó Laighléis
(ISBN 0-9532777-9-8)

This acclaimed collection looks at the rise, the fall and the versatility of the human spirit, touching, as it does, on almost every aspect of human trial and existence. Though unflinchingly hard-hitting, it is utterly compelling and written with great insight and sensitivity. Ó Laighléis' greatest gift is that he is a masterful story-teller.

"This combination of style and tone provides a maturity which rarely characterises writing targeted mainly at a teenage readership ... It deserves the widest possible audience."
Robert Dunbar, *The Irish Times*

"Always there is an appropriate honed-down style that presents the narratives in crystal clear detail ... Not just a book for teenagers, but for everyone who appreciates first-class writing."
Tony Hickey, *Village*

"Ó Laighléis is not one for the soft option. He deals unflinchingly with major social issues that affect all our lives and deals with them with profound insight and intelligence ... It is Ó Laighléis' creative imagination that gives the collection its undeniable power. The economy of his prose allows for no authorial moralising."
Books Ireland

"Ecstasy and other stories is brilliantly written and an eye-opener for us all as to what could happen if life takes that one wrong turn. Ré Ó Laighléis is a master of his craft."
Geraldine Molloy, *The Big Issues*

"Ecstasy is evocative of the filmography of Ken Loach, and its minimalistic story-telling, with its sparse and essential style, constitutes an extraordinarily expressive force."
Mondadori, Milan, Italy (publishers)

"The short stories of Ecstasy ... take us, in the Irish context, into new thematic territories and, more importantly, pay their characters (and, by extension, their readers) the compliment of allowing them to live with the consequences of their own choices: complex circumstances are always seen to defy easy outcomes."
Books, *The Irish Times Weekend Supplement*

ALSO AVAILABLE FROM MÓINÍN

TERROR ON THE BURREN
by
Ré Ó Laighléis
(ISBN 0-9532777-0-4)

This multiple award-winning and critically acclaimed novel is a superlative mix of the supernatural and the real. Set against the archaeological and geological richness of the Burren landscape in Ireland's County Clare, the author weaves a mesmeric and multi-layered tale of barbarity and beauty, of the imaginative and intrigue, of good and evil.

"Measured, even against his own already high standards, Ré Ó Laighléis has given us an exceptional work of beauty and terror here. This, quite simply, stands apart." **C.J. Haughey, former Taoiseach**

"Another example of Ó Laighléis' shining creations ... Undoubtedly, Ó Laighléis is a gifted writer and we wait with hungry curiosity to see what he will come up with next." **Tom Widger, *The Sunday Tribune***

"You'll never look at the Burren in the same way after you read this tale ... Anyone even slightly intrigued by alternatives to the 20th century's blueprint for living will find this account of life in 200 BC enchanting ... The whole saga unfolds within a slim 114 pages, with the mystical beauty of the Burren permeating every page." **Sharon Diviney, *Ireland on Sunday***

"This is an unusual work of rich and cinematographic prose, a work of excellence in the fantasy genre and one which bears the scope of The Mists of Avalon.*"* **Gabriel Rosenstock, Writer**

"Though ostensibly set on the Burren in the period of prehistory, Ó Laighléis' horrific story of destruction is inextricably connected to more recent murky happenings." **Prof. Mícheál Mac Craith,
National University of Ireland, Galway**

"A brilliant and fascinating read, which will hold you enthralled to the very end." **Geraldine Molloy, *The Big Issues***

"This is epic story-telling at its very best." **Tony Hickey, *Village***

BATTLE FOR THE BURREN
by
Ré Ó Laighléis
(ISBN 978-0-9554079-1-8)

It is 1317 AD, some 1,500 years since the visionary Sobhartan fought her epic battle against Evil on the shores of Loughrask. Though long since dead, her spirit is embodied in the old blind monk, Benignus, who, like her, has been both blessed and cursed with the gift of vision. He is an elder of the community of Cistercians who occupy the monastery at Corcomroe on the Burren's beautiful, yet unforgiving foothills. Set against the great wars of the divided factions of the Clan O'Brien, the power of Evil has found a willing home in the heart and soul of the dark and sinister Feardorcha, a lieutenant in the forces of Prince Donough O'Brien. The opposing forces of Donough and his cousin, Dermot, are making for the holy place at Corcomroe, where, once and for all, the bloodiest of battles will be fought to determine supremacy within the Clan O'Brien. And bloody it will be, and such will be the ensuing slaughter that devastation of its kind will be unprecedented.

This is the backdrop against which young Iarla O'Brien, son of Dermot, conducts his secretive and passion-filled relationship with Sorcha, daughter of Mahon, one of Prince Donough's most ardent and loyal supporters. Though fired with love and hope for a future together, the young lovers are all too aware of the divisions between their families and of the dangers that lie ahead. Their fates are outside of them and will ultimately be determined by the powers of Good and Evil. An epic tale of love, of fear and darkness.

"His characters are described and their speech declaimed in formal, sometimes florid prose, but this is tempered by the author's loving descriptions of nature and some powerful battle scenes."
Elizabeth McGuane, The Sunday Business Post

"The two O'Brien cousins, Prince Dermot and Prince Donough, who will confront each other in one of the bloodiest O'Brien battles ever, is the backdrop to a story of love, fear and powers of darkness that sweep the reader from one plateau to another ... I can highly recommend this book to all ..." **Lord Inchiquin, Sir Conor O'Brien, Chieftain of the Clan O'Brien, Prince of Thomond**

HEART OF BURREN STONE
A collection of short stories
by
Ré Ó Laighléis

National and international award-winning author Ré Ó Laighléis gives us a collection that is disturbingly provocative, yet permeated throughout by a humane and perceptive sensitivity. His stories alternate between the serious and witty. Set against both urban and rural backgrounds, these stories range in location from England to the United States and from France to Ireland North and South, with a concentration on the Burren.

Ó Laighléis is equally adept whether handling the loss of childhood innocence in cosmopolitan Dublin or remotest rural Ireland, the depravity that, at times, replaces such innocence in adult years, or the twists in life that determine happiness and misery. His characters bear all the frailty and vulnerability that epitomise the difficulty of survival in contemporary society.

Whether the tragicomedy of two nine-year-olds arguing their political corners on the North of Ireland's Garvaghy Road, the conniving roguery of a Burren publisher or the pain-filled dilemma of a dying cancer patient in a Boston hospital appealing to be assisted on his way – there is an unnerving universality to Ó Laighléis' writing.

ALSO AVAILABLE FROM MÓINÍN

THE GREAT BOOK OF THE SHAPERS:
A right kick up in the Arts
by
Ré Ó Laighléis
(ISBN 0-9532777-8-X)

In a world where there are fewer true artists than there are mere pretenders and where the ordinary citizen is disenfranchised, yet has to subsidise the indulgences and affectations of poseurs and shapers, these would-be artists are so far up their own ends that they are coming out of their mouths – and sometimes, it would nearly seem, out of others' mouths.

Ó Laighléis bursts the bubble on the 'let's-say-nothing' culture of pretence, as the ubiquitous and ever-overseeing Fly tee-hees his way throughout the hilarity of it all.

This satirical look at a pretentiousness in the arts that feeds upon itself really is 'let's-call-a-spade-a-shovel' territory.

"This latest novel, his eighth, again highlights Ó Laighléis' remarkable versatility."

CORKnow

"It is a farcical tirade against the hangers-on, the spoofers, the plámásers and the lickspittles that gravitate towards the arts: hoisted up on their own petard, they succeed in disenfranchising both themselves and the man-on-the-street from the arts world."

Mark Keane, *The Clare People*

"Ó Laighléis satirises the pretentious in the hope that some sanity may return to our appreciation of what is culturally sound, and that we judge things for what they really are and not what they pretend to be."

'Book of the Week', *Galway Independent*

"Art and art form are lost, while characters lose themselves with their own sense of importance."

Aingeal Ní Mhurchú, *The Southern Star*